parABnormal Magazine

December 2023

Edited by H. David Blalock

parABnormal Magazine
December 2023

All rights reserved. No part of this book may be reproduced or transmitted in any form or by any means, electronic or mechanical, including photocopying or recording or by any information storage and retrieval systems, without expressed written consent of the authors and/or artists.

parABnormal Magazine is a work of fiction. Names, characters, places, and incidents are products of the authors' imaginations. Any resemblance to actual events or persons, living or dead, is entirely coincidental.

Story and illustration copyrights owned by the respective authors and artists.

Cover illustration "First Snowfall" by Mat Kaminski
Cover design by Laura Givens
First Printing, December 2023
Hiraeth Publishing
http://www.hiraethsffh.com/

Visit http://www.hiraethsffh.com/ for online science fiction, fantasy, horror, scifaiku, and more. Support the small, independent press...

Vol. V, No. 4, Issue #20   December 2023

parABnormal Magazine is published quarterly on the 15th day of March, June, September, and December in the United States of America by Hiraeth Publishing, P.O. Box 1248, Tularosa, NM, 88352. Copyright 2022 by Hiraeth Publishing. All rights revert to authors and artists upon publication except as noted in selected individual contracts. Nothing may be reproduced in whole or in part without written permission from the authors and artists. Any similarity between places and persons mentioned in the fiction or semi-fiction and real places or persons living or dead is coincidental. Writers and artists guidelines are available online at www.hiraethsffh.com. Guidelines are also available upon request from Hiraeth Publishing, P.O. Box 1248, Tularosa, NM, 88352, if request is accompanied by a self-addressed #10 envelope with a first-class US stamp. Editor: H David Blalock.

Contents

Stories
7	Azrael by Elizabeth Donald
18	The Man At Table Twelve by Stetson Ray
34	The Hungry Swamp by Tom Howard
53	Blood Beach by Gregory Jeffers
71	Act of Creation by Donna J. W. Munro

Poems
33	The Sonnet the Ghost Wrote on My Mirror While I Showered by Marcus Wahlbring
52	Evening in the Infirmary by Rob E. Boley
70	Spring Brings Everything Back to Life by Renee Crowley
81	Warning by Sarah Cannavo
82	Cry of the Banshee by Denise Noe

Articles
83	Great and Terrible: An Examination of Jonathan Edwards', "Sinners in the Hands of an Angry God" Through the Lens of Cosmic Horror by Anthony Perconti
90	Plunging into the Mystery of Automatic or Mediumistic Art & Artists by Sonali Roy
100	Joyce Carol Oates's Second Exploration of Grotesquerie: *The Collector of Hearts* by Denise Noe

Illustrations
52	Nature's Horns by Sonali Roy
82	Funeral of Mankind by Sonali Roy

A Little Help, Please

In the world of the small indie press we fight a never-ending battle for attention to our work, as writers and in publishing. Here's an example: big publishers [you know who they are] have gobs of $$$ that they can devote to advertising and marketing. Here at Hiraeth Publishing, our advertising budget consists of the deposits for whatever soda bottles and aluminum cans we can find alongside the highways. Anti-littering laws make our task even more difficult . . . J

That's where YOU come in. YOU are our best promoter. YOU are the one who can tell others about us. Just send 'em to our website, tell them about our store. That's all. Just that.

Of course, we don't mind if you talk us up. We're pretty good, you know. We have some award-winning and award-nominated writers and artists, plus other voices well-deserving to be heard [not everyone wins awards, right?] but our publications are read-worthy nevertheless.

That number once again is:

www.hiraethsffh.com

Friend us on Facebook at Hiraeth Publishing

Follow us on Twitter at @HiraethPublish1

What???

No subscription to parABnormal Magazine??

We can fix that . . .

Just go here and order:

https://www.hiraethsffh.com/product-page/parabnormal-magazine-subscription

...also makes a great gift any time of the year

Azrael
Elizabeth Donald

"You die now."

The young man blinks at me as I hover over his rickety wooden table in the noisy coffeehouse, and he drops the stack of cards he is dealing to his pretty blond girlfriend. She is distracted by her phone, a frown creasing a line between her eyebrows as she pokes at it and pays little attention to their card game, her boyfriend, or to me.

"Excuse me?" He is about twenty years old, in perfect physical shape wearing a college T-shirt and baseball cap worn backwards. Because I am what I am, I know that he plays pickup basketball three times a week at his university gym, and the rest of the time he devotes his energy to enjoying the body of the young woman sitting across from him, sipping a latte. He is planning one such aerobic session as soon as they get back to the dorm this evening.

But it has been a long day, and I have little patience for this boy's mundane moment. I have a job to do, and I am going to get it done if it kills me. So to speak.

"You die now," I repeat, and go on my way. I used to say it in Latin. They didn't understand it then, either.

The young man stares after me, and I hear him ask his girlfriend if she'd heard what I said. She hadn't, of course, and he said never mind. It doesn't matter. No one but him would have heard me in the loud, crowded coffeehouse where a dozen people wait for their lattes and incomprehensible music drifts from speakers hidden behind nonsensical art.

Even if it had been silent, no one would have heard me or seen me except the young man himself, who will crash his motorcycle today on the way back to the dorm. He doesn't wear a helmet, because he is twenty and thinks himself immortal. No more horizontal aerobics for him. The girl will live.

As I make my way to the coffeehouse door, an old man brushes past me, moving slowly toward the counter in the hopes of a cup of Darjeeling. Cancer, and within a few months, but still too early for the pronunciation.

I step onto the sidewalk, and a heart disease passes me, chatting pleasantly with a murder. That is an interesting confluence, so I linger for a second. The young brunette throws back her head and laughs, the shiny new engagement ring glinting on her finger as her fiancé kisses her cheek. The late afternoon sun shines down on them, and they are a bright glittering spot of joy and contentment.

Four years from now he will strangle her in a fit a jealousy after he finds a voicemail on her phone he considers suspicious, which turns out to be completely innocent. He will weep when they sentence him to prison for the rest of his life, and he will be beaten and tortured in unspeakable ways for nine years before early heart disease claims him. Just as well.

I have seen it happen literally millions of times, in every way it can possibly happen to a human. I have pronounced infants in their cribs and homeless men indistinguishable beneath their filthy blankets under the highway overpass. I have worked overtime in mass shootings and hospital wards and vicious explosions and war zones. It's all the same, whether it's a foxhole or a nursery. It's all according to the Plan, and my job is simple.

I walk further down the street, passing an embolism six years out. She is a thirty-something mother struggling with an infant in a stroller as her toddler whines beside her. The embolism will strike while she's waiting in the pickup line at the baby's elementary school, and her foot will slide off the brake, sending her car slow-rolling into the side of the building. The teachers will scramble all the kids out of the way, and I will have no one else to pronounce that day.

Assuming it is me, of course — it could be one of my brethren. There are many of us, and we wander in the spaces between people, always present. Sometimes you shiver when we pass, and you don't really see us, not the way you see each other. But you think about us in a passing moment, and know that one of us has passed near you, a finger of ice on the back of your neck. We're not precisely invisible, you know. You just choose not to see us.

The embolism's toddler son will turn to drugs as a teenager and die of an overdose during his second year of college. The baby will survive to be a great-grandmother before her stroke. At her last moment, as her weeping husband and children hold her hands and surround her with love, she will remember the face of her long-dead mother kissing her goodnight.

I walk past the courthouse, where four lung cancers in a row are lighting up beside the no-smoking sign and chatting with a drunk-driving car wreck. At the corner deli, another cancer stepped out with takeout, his lovely Alzheimer's wife following behind him as she puts her wallet back into her purse.

No one looks at me.

I don't have horns and a pitchfork, I'm not a demon and I have no interest in the apocalypse beyond whatever the Plan has to say. The most intimidating thing about me is my long trench coat, which is my latest attempt to blend in. We've tried a lot of different looks through the years — you've probably read about them in dusty books or seen them in the movies. Management doesn't care how we do the job, as long as the pronunciation gets done in a reasonable period of time before the Plan requires the death to occur.

There's a system.

I walk among you every day, and I know how you'll die and when. I don't make deals. I just pronounce, and most of the time I'm forgotten before it happens. Already the motorcycle wreck in the coffeehouse has forgotten me, and his last card game is nearly done. She's winning.

It's not magic. There's no spell preventing you from acknowledging me. You just don't want to admit that I exist. As though life is any less important because it ends.

I drift onward along my schedule. The Plan is busy today. There's an angry young man named Devin, loading a dozen guns and hiding them in a gym bag. I'm headed for him, of course, but not just him. There are seven others he will take with him today.

Devin thinks he's going to the public library, but right about now he's changing course. He's scared off when he sees a police car parked out front of the library, and he's diverting to the grocery store. The police officer inside the squad car is just eating his lunch, of course, and has no idea that Devin passed the library because of him. Inside the library there are twelve children at after-school story hour, and my shadow has passed them by simply because the Plan indicated that the police officer will choose this spot to eat his cheeseburger. Everything has been set down in advance, even those last-minute whims of so-called Fate.

I don't write the Plan, either. That's Management's job. It's quite dull, really.

I catch up to Devin in the parking lot of the grocery store. He's sitting in his beat-up Ford pickup, his hand on the duffel bag, a moment of indecision. I can't change his mind, of course. He chooses not to see me, because he thinks of me as something beautiful, some glorious angel he has sought on at least two occasions, not a nondescript guy in a trench coat standing behind his truck, giving pronunciation.

He's going to be so disappointed.

All those guns in the duffel, but Devin grabs only one, stuffing it inside his jacket. He probably could have snuck the duffel into the library, but it's a crowded afternoon at the grocery store and he fears interference. He's walking across the parking lot toward the store entrance.

I drift after him, passing a man carrying flowers and a box of candy out of the store. He's in trouble at home, having spent half his paycheck at the casino last weekend, but she will forgive him and ask him to mend his ways, simply relieved that he missed the horrors waiting inside the grocery store by five minutes. He will abide by her wishes for a while, but he will continue to sneak back to the boats for the next ten years until the car accident, when we will meet again.

Devin passes through the doorway into the produce section, where a worker named Steven is stocking pineapples in a large bin toward the front under a giant yellow SALE! sign. Steven is graying and bald, a heart attack six years from now who always meant to go for a management job, but never had the bravery to actually apply. He's joking with his teenage coworker, Chris, who is checking the avocados for bad ones. Avocados rot so quickly from the inside.

Devin is loitering by the organic greens, his hand lightly resting on the gun in his jacket pocket. He still hasn't made up his mind, but feeling the handgun there comforts him. *I could shoot them all right now,* he's thinking. Of Alexandra, the young mother with the toddler in her cart - Timmy - loading up on apples and tangerines. Of Linda, the woman in the hairnet taking a potato salad order at the deli counter from Doris, the old lady who can't quite hear her. Of Steven and Chris by the pineapples.

He is relishing that power, the invisible sword he holds over them, the thin strand of life that lies between the blades of the scissors he holds. None of them thinks they will die today, and it's up to him whether they live or not. Or so he believes. It's all in the Plan.

A young woman moves past me, leaving the cereals and canned goods to enter the produce section under a wave of tinny pop music. Her attention is on Devin, but she's being careful not to look too closely at him. She's not on my list for today, but I drift closer out of curiosity.

Her name is Juliet, and touching her mind is like skating over a frozen lake, a thin scrum of cracked ice covering dark, rotten water. No, that isn't right. It is worse than cold. It is empty, an abyss deadening her from the inside out, killing the life at the center of her into morose silence.

She feels nothing, and craves feeling. She has tried to fill that abyss with any number of things. Cutting her skin in places where it would not show and the bleeding would not be too deep. Grunting, meaningless encounters in hotel rooms with a man who slipped his ring back on before he left. Drowning herself in cheap bourbon until she passes out, only to wake alone and empty again.

Juliet's favorite place is the bridge over the river, on the edge of town. It's an old bridge and they don't let people drive across it anymore, but you can walk, and Juliet trudges to the center and thinks about jumping. She looks at the cold water and the rocks far below her and wonders if she would feel when she struck them.

The bridge fills her mind all the time, even when she isn't there, even when she's lying underneath the man, hoping his penetration will finally drive the bridge from her mind completely. She urges him to be rough, to be hard on her, and for a moment or two it drives the bridge from her mind. But then he withdraws and it consumes her again, the emptiness of the abyss and the roiling water beneath the bridge.

Juliet is hardly the first I'd felt with that darkness inside, as some of those who intentionally seek me out succeed. She doesn't know what Devin is planning. But she draws near them nonetheless, as if the colorless waves within her are drawn to the screaming fire inside him.

Alexandra and little Timmy leave the produce section. Sandra, a trim middle-aged woman in a nice suit, enters in search of a decent pomegranate. Time to work.

Distracted by Juliet, I barely have time to mutter my pronunciation before Devin's first bullet strikes Sandra in the center of her back, knocking her down into the rack of lemons and limes in a spill of bright colors. Yellow. Green. Red.

Steven hits the ground fast. He was in Afghanistan, and now he can't remember if this is a grocery store or a market in Kabul, but he has the presence of mind to drag a stunned Chris to the floor with him and shove him behind the cherry tomatoes. Steven's hand flies to his belt, but there is no service weapon there. It has been seventeen years.

Doris is screaming beside the deli counter as she falls behind the dubious cover of the cheese display, and Linda the hairnet woman has disappeared behind the glass case, frantically dialing 911 on her cell phone as she hides behind the fried chicken. Elsewhere someone is screaming, and I wonder who it might be.

I'm supposed to collect six more today besides Sandra among the limes. But something is happening here, a strange veil over my sight like mist. This isn't the way the Plan is written. Something has changed — for the first time in as long as I can remember, something new.

"Active shooter!" a voice announces over the intercom, and the screaming doubles, triples in aisles far away from Devin and the people in the produce section. The overhead lights all shut off. At the other end of the store, I know people are abandoning carts and running for the doors on the far side of the checkout counters, far away from Devin. The only light now is coming from the emergency spotlights above the exit signs and the late-afternoon sunlight streaming in from outside.

A checkout clerk appears for a second, running from her station to the door nearest us, silhouetted for a moment against the sun. Devin takes a shot but misses, shattering the glass. There is no pronunciation to be made.

Juliet steps in front of Devin. I can feel her excitement — *at last*. Devin is like a gift to her. The gnawing cold, that hole she can never fill, she believes he will wash it away from her in blood and pain and that will be better than the nothing.

She's not on my list. The Plan does not include her.

Devin is shouting something at her, and she reaches for the gun.

He shoots Juliet in the midsection, and then again, over and over and until she falls over, knocking a stand of raspberries into a reddened halo around her head in the shadows on the floor.

Her breathing stills, silent on the floor.

I cannot move. She is not in the Plan. I can't even sense when she is supposed to die, and there is a strange gray veil over my sight that makes everything vague and insubstantial. Six more, there are supposed to be six more, and suddenly I can't see any of them. I cannot recall ever experiencing this feeling in my long life, this not-knowing. The same uncertainty, blind faith stumbling about in the darkness, that is the average human existence. The Plan has always been innate to me, surfacing as I summoned it, with every step of every day, month, year, millennium laid out for me.

I have no Plan. I cannot move. How am I to know who to pronounce and who to pass by if there is no Plan? And if there is no Plan, what does that mean for the system? Is it just me, or all my brethren as well? What will Management say? Is there even anyone in Management now?

My mind swirled with all these questions, dizzy and frozen at the same time, and with a tiny thread of excitement, bright and glittering like a strand of gold amidst wool. For the first time, no Plan. No instructions. As though I were free.

Devin has run out of bullets. He scrambles through his pockets for more, reloading the gun and wishing he had brought the duffel after all.

I have no idea who will die now.

Steven takes the opportunity to push Chris toward the nearest door, and Chris makes a break for it, slipping a little on the broken glass. Devin aims for him, but Steven lobs a goddamn pineapple at him and the shot goes wild. Chris scrambles through the shattered door, and I know he will marry his high school girlfriend and die of cancer as a great-grandfather.

There's still a Plan, then? I shake my head, trying to dispel the fog, this uncertainty that surrounds me.

Devin is agitated, shooting into piles of fruit, but Steven has wisely hit the ground again, searching the fallen produce for anything remotely resembling a weapon.

That's when Juliet rises from the floor and rushes at Devin, grappling with him for the gun. It goes off twice more, whining harmlessly off the floor, and she manages to wrest it from his hands, shoving him back into the greens.

She stands tall, aiming the gun at him as Devin screams in wordless frustration.

The room spins under my feet as though on a merry-go-round, tilting back and forth and threatening to push me off my feet.

Juliet pulls the trigger, and Devin falls backward. Into his own abyss. I pronounced him ten minutes ago, in the parking lot.

The veil shifts again, an almost nauseating turbulence as though I am walking through an airplane in high winds. The walls of the grocery store spin in a ludicrous cyclone of blood and fruit, and the floor lurches under my feet. I reach out, again, for the Plan.

I no longer have seven people to collect. Sandra among the limes and Devin himself will be my only pronunciations here.

The Plan changed. But it never changes.

I step closer to Juliet, who stands with her head bowed in the strange half-light coming from the shattered door, the center of that glittering gold strand that changed the Plan. The gun is still in her hand, and she thinks of using it, but knows that it is no use. Her shirt is torn to pieces from Devin's bullets, but her flesh beneath it is smooth and unmarked. That rush of fear and exhilaration has faded from her, and the horror and sorrow she feels at the sight of Devin's bloodied body is welling up.

The abyss is full, but it is full of blood and guilt and grief and all sorts of screaming horrors she had never imagined. It is full of the madness in Devin's eyes, the fear and confusion as the bullet struck him, the nightmarish slow-motion fall backward at her hand.

Now she knows there is something worse than feeling nothing.

"Who are you?" I ask. The words are strange in my mouth, though I form them easily. I have said nothing to humans for so long besides my pronunciation. It is possible these are my first new-spoken words since I gave up the Latin. I cannot quite recall.

I know she will not hear me. She is not on my list, she will not choose to see me.

But she lifts her head and stares straight at me, as no one ever does, not Sandra or Devin or even the boy in the coffeehouse.

"Who do you say I am?" she asks.

The Man at Table Twelve
Stetson Ray

"Table ten says these are overcooked," Beth Foster said, and slid a plate through the serving window. "I need two more eggs—over-easy this time." The row of line cooks glared at her like cavemen preparing to drive away an unwanted intruder. Beth picked up two plates that belonged to table eleven and scurried away.

The diner was busy—especially for a Sunday morning—but Beth only had three tables left to serve before she was free to leave. She dropped off table eleven's food: steak and eggs for the man, a bacon and cheese omelet for the woman.

"Eggs for ten," a line cook called.

Beth grabbed the plate and took it to table ten. The old man sitting in the booth didn't seem happy—not that Beth expected him to be. She didn't know the man's name, but he came in pretty often, and nothing was ever good enough for him. Complainers were common, and Beth knew the type well. No matter how good the service, no matter how delicious the food, the man still would've found something to complain about. Complainers complain, and she'd heard it all before:

"This syrup is too sweet."

"This egg doesn't have enough yolk, and too much white."

"There's a hair in my hashbrowns," a man with a bushy beard once told her, shocked to find a familiar looking hair sitting *on top* of his food.

Beth flashed her brightest smile and apologized as sincerely as she could, but the man at table ten didn't look happy with his eggs. He grumbled something and picked up his fork and Beth left him to stew in his misery. She checked on table eleven (they were doing fine, the man's steak was cooked correctly, they didn't need refills), then went to her third table.

The man at table twelve was alone. He was taking up an entire booth just to drink coffee, and had been sipping from his cup for hours. Beth wasn't sure how, but they had gotten off on the wrong foot, and every time she refilled his cup things got a little worse. Even though twenty percent of his bill would be roughly a quarter, Beth had put on a fake smile and remained friendly. Sometimes that was just part of the job.

"Need a refill?" Beth asked, smiling.

Without turning his neck, the man looked at her and said, "No. I'm fine."

"Let me know if you need anything else," she said, and walked away.

Knowing she would graduate college soon and never have to deal with another complainer or coffee squatter again kept her going most days, but if she was honest with herself, the thought of the tip money drying up frightened her. Nobody was footing the bill for her education; it was up to her alone to pay her bills. She needed the tips that table ten and eleven would surely leave, but she couldn't stay much longer.

She had an appointment to keep.

For too long she had put off breaking up with her college fling: a boy named Mike who she barely liked enough to keep around. Mike was sweet and easy to look at, but he wasn't her future. They would both be moving away in May and Beth thought it best to end things before it got messy; no part of her wanted to spend the rest of her life with Mike, or wait for their soon to be long distance relationship to implode. They had agreed to meet at a local park at noon, and being held hostage by some guy who had nothing better to do but drink coffee was not part of the plan.

Tables ten and eleven paid their bills and left.

Time was running out.

Beth had to figure out a way to make the man at twelve leave.

Standing behind the counter beside the cash register, she watched him. He wasn't reading a newspaper or thumbing his phone; he wasn't even drinking coffee anymore. The man didn't look like a weirdo, just an average looking guy in his late thirties, but something about him put her off. The way he looked at her every time she refilled his coffee was unsettling.

An old man wearing a suit walked in, followed by an equally old woman wearing a floor length dress. Beth didn't have much longer. The Baptists were coming. It was time for twelve to go. If she didn't leave before the after-church crowd began to pour in, she'd be stuck for at least three more hours.

"I thought you left," an older woman named Linda said, the most senior waitress and acting manager of the diner.

"Not yet," Beth said.

"Still waitin' on twelve?" Linda asked.

"Yes," Beth answered, and another older couple wearing nice clothes walked in.

Linda said, "It's like a Band-Aid, honey: you gotta tear it off fast."

Beth took a deep breath and walked over to twelve and slapped the bill down on the table like a gambler playing a winning hand.

"Is there anything else I can get for you before you go?" Beth asked, pleading with her eyes.

The man didn't acknowledge her in any way. She wondered how long she could keep standing there, holding her smile. It looked like gears were turning inside the man's mind, but he said nothing. Beth wasn't expecting to be stonewalled, and it caused her temper to flare. It was getting late, and her patience was gone.

"Would you like a to-go cup?" she asked, and refreshed her smile.

His head craned upward and his eyes met hers.

Beth had seen some strange things during her time at the diner, but she'd never seen a grown man cry. Maybe a few kids here and there, but never an adult. Tears dripped off the man's face and landed on the table. Still, he said nothing.

"I'm so sorry," she said automatically. "Is there... anything I can do for you?"

He wiped his face with a napkin.

Beth just stood there.

"Can I ask you something, Beth?"

"Sure," she said, and only later would she realize that she had forgotten to put her name tag on that morning.

"Does everything seem off to you? Like the whole world is a little different than it was yesterday?"

"Not that I've noticed."

If the man was trying to be funny, Beth didn't get the joke.

"I thought not," he said. "I think I'm the one who's out of place."

After a few seconds of silence, Beth said, "Is there anything—"

"You don't recognize me?" the man interrupted.

Beth's brain kicked into overdrive and began sorting through the faces of her regular customers like a motorized Rolodex.

There was Doris and Milton, the kind, elderly couple that came in twice a week who sometimes tried to hook her up with their grandson, but were otherwise nice people. There was Buddy, a quiet man that clearly liked his favorite waitress a little too much, but was harmless. One or two professors from the college she knew by name. And a dozen local regulars, little old men that could've been anyone's grandfather. Some treated Beth like she was family, and she genuinely enjoyed serving some of her customers.

But Beth had never seen the man at table twelve before.

"I'm sorry," she said, trying to sound congenial. "We get so busy it's hard to keep track of who's coming and going." She smiled again and made a sound that only vaguely resembled a laugh. Her platitudes had no effect on the man. He was staring at Beth as though she were the cause of every problem he'd ever had.

He said, "That's what I thought," and one of his hands left the table and wrestled with something in his pocket.

Beth deflated. He was finally leaving. Soon his billfold would make an appearance, the check would close, and she might even have time to change clothes before meeting Mike at the park. But instead of retrieving a square of leather from his pocket, the man pulled out a pistol and laid it on the table. He did it so very casually that at first, it didn't strike Beth as unusual.

She should've ran, but that moment came and went, leaving her standing there frozen. She looked down at the gun, hypnotized. Suddenly the diner didn't seem so loud anymore.

"Sit down," the man said, his hand resting on top of the gun.

None of her prior waitressing experiences had prepared her for such a situation. Beth had received no relevant training, and none of the pre-scripted lines she had said a thousand times before seemed applicable. No one in the diner could see the weapon; Beth was blocking the booth from view with her body. No one could hear the man either; he was speaking quietly.

The man gently tapped the gun on the table.

I said, "*Sit down.*"

Beth slid into the booth and hoped that Linda or someone else—anyone else—would notice that something wasn't right. But that could take a minute. Table twelve was in the corner of the diner, and there was no one in the booth behind Beth.

"I thought I could come here and drink some coffee and pretend that everything was fine, but you haven't made that easy, have you?" The man spoke through gritted teeth. "You just keep on with the questions, the same ones every time, just rubbing it in a little more with every word."

Belt felt tears coming.

The man was nuts.

Full on crazy.

She had learned how to deal with the occasional disgruntled customer and late-night drunk who thought they had a chance with her, but the man sitting across the table from her was dangerous, unhinged. The word *hostage* floated through her mind like an out of control blimp. She didn't know which was worse: looking into the man's eyes, or looking at the pistol.

"Don't worry," he said, catching her eyes on the gun, "I'm not going to hurt you." He slid the pistol off the table into his lap, but kept his hand on it. "I just wanna talk to you for a minute. Is that alright?"

"Yes," she breathed, tears running down her face.

"You want to hear something crazy?"

She looked at him.

He looked at her.

She said nothing.

"Nearly every Sunday for the past two and a half years, me and my family have come to this little grease bucket for breakfast, and you know who our waitress was every time?"

"I don't know."

"Of course not," the man said, looking disgusted. He looked out of the window beside the booth and his eyes glazed over, like a strong memory had returned to him. He turned back to her and said, "There's one waitress in particular who my kids absolutely adore. See, I've got a six year old boy and a three year old girl, and they won't even think about eating their waffle's unless you are the one who brings them to our table."

Beth sucked in a lungful of air. Apparently she'd been holding her breath since she sat down.

"I can get my manager," she said for some reason, but the man went on like she hadn't said anything.

"You know, it's not so much my little girl, Rosemary, who likes to come here. It's mostly my son, Eli. Guess he's got a thing for college girls."

Some invisible force was keeping Beth planted in the booth. She was afraid to move, afraid to even blink.

"Remember when you let it slip that you had a boyfriend and Eli cried?" The man slapped his hand on the table and laughed. Beth jerked and almost bolted. The man didn't seem to notice. Now he was smiling at Beth like she was an old friend.

"What-is-his-name, uh...Mitch, or no...Mike, right?"

Beth felt violated enough to get angry.

"How do you know my boyfriend's name? Have you been following me? Is that what this is? Are you some kind of pervert stalker or something?"

"No, it's nothing like that," he said, and took a drink of his coffee. "I've got some issues, sure, but I'm no pervert, and I've never cheated on my wife."

Beth turned her head, but no one was watching them. A thought flashed to life in her mind: maybe if she could get the man mad enough—though not mad enough to shoot her—he would do something to get someone's attention.

She spoke before she thought.

"I bet you hit her though, right?"

The man slammed his hand down on the table and everything on it bounced and clanged.

"That was one time," the man growled, fire in his eyes, "*and she deserved it.*"

"What about your kids? Did they deserve it too?"

"I've never hit my kids, Beth. *Never.*" He narrowed his eyes at her, his face red. Then the anger left him and he said, "Until last night. But that was a mistake. I didn't mean for it to happen that way. It wasn't my fault. I've got temper problems. I..." He trailed off, not really looking at Beth, but looking through her. "I still can't believe it, but I killed them, Beth. I killed my fam—" His voice broke and his face contorted and he laid his head on the table and cried.

Customers were starting to look, but no one seemed concerned yet. Beth knew what would happen if she ran: the man would shoot her in the back before she took a third step. The butter knife lying on the edge of the table wouldn't be a much better option. There was no way she could kill him with such a pathetic weapon. Again, she'd just end up getting shot.

Linda was watching Beth with her hands on her hips, visibly confused. The old waitress held up her wrist and tapped her watch. Her lips said, "*Church rush.*" Beth made her hand into the shape of a phone and stuck it against her head. Linda looked confused, but Beth didn't have time to give any more signals. She quickly turned back to the man as he raised his head from the table. He didn't bother to wipe the tears and snot from his face.

He said, "I left right after I killed them and spent a few hours driving around trying to clear my head, and that's when I decided what I was going to do." He blew his nose into a napkin. "I decided I couldn't live without my family, so I went straight home to end it—punish myself for what I did to them. But wouldn't you know it, our house wasn't there anymore. It had been replaced by a new home, totally different. I knocked on the door and some lady answered. I tried to ask her some questions but she slammed the door on me." The man raised the gun and laid it on the table and Beth's heart rate skyrocketed. "I thought about doing it there, in my car, but then I decided to come here and drink some coffee and reminisce for a while, you know, try to think about the good times. But that was a bad idea." He sniffled and blew his nose again. "I don't know what's going on, and I didn't mean to involve you in all this, Beth. I shouldn't be here. I know I shouldn't be here. I can feel it. It feels…*wrong*."

Beth turned her head. Linda was staring, her eyes wide, holding a phone against her ear.

"If you wanna know the truth, I had this wild idea that maybe they'd be here, you know? I thought maybe if I sat here long enough they'd show up and we could eat breakfast and pretend like nothing ever happened." He shook his head and looked out the window again. "But they're never coming back. I know that now."

Beth didn't know what to say. She watched him, waiting for whatever came next.

He looked at her and said, "You know, I'm really hoping this isn't real. Maybe it's some kind of nightmare. I'd do just about anything to wake up at home in my bed—God I hope that's what happens."

"Sir, the police are on the way," Linda announced, and the whole diner went silent and everyone looked at table twelve. "Don't do anything you'll regret."

"I'm sorry. Tell everybody I'm sorry. I love my family, I just made a mistake."

The man looked much older than he had an hour before.

Beth desperately wanted to help him, but she didn't know how.

She was no longer afraid, only confused.

"You were always a good waitress, Beth," the man said, then stuck the gun under his chin and pulled the trigger.

***

It only took a few minutes to wash the dead man's blood out of her hair, but Beth's ears rang for a week. In the days following the unexpected suicide, she had to answer a thousand questions. The police asked the same things over and over again; it was maddening.

About a month later, Beth found herself answering yet another call from a detective named John Weber. He was about her mother's age and looked tired all the time. He often called Beth to update her on the case and ask new questions, but all the police had learned so far about the man at table twelve was his name:

David Anderson.

It didn't ring a bell, and despite his story, Beth was certain she had never served him before.

There was apprehension in Weber's voice, and he kept stumbling over his words.

"Is something wrong?" Beth asked, pushing the phone against her ear.

Weber sighed and said, "What I'm about to say might sound a bit odd, but about four years ago, David Anderson killed his son and wife and set his house on fire. Until recently, we thought he'd killed himself shortly after starting the fire. According to his records, Anderson had some significant anger issues, so it all made sense—looked like a standard murder-suicide."

Beth made an odd noise.

Weber kept talking.

"See, there were three bodies in the house and one of them matched Anderson in every way—even the dental records and the fingerprints. We're still looking into how he did it, but the working theory is that he either killed a third person, or somehow got a hold of a dead body, but either way, he successfully planted a body in his house and faked his death—until now that is."

Beth said, "He—David—he told me he had a daughter named Rosemary. What about her?"

"No, he only had one child, a boy," Weber said, and she could hear papers rustling. "You sure the name was Rosemary?"

"Yes, I'm positive. I remember everything he said." Every second Beth had spent sitting at table twelve had been permanently burned into her memory. "I'm sure I told you that."

"Yes, I see it here in the report," Weber said, and the paper-rustling stopped. "Looks like Anderson's mother was named Rosemary. She died a few months after the fire. Cancer."

Scattered thoughts blew about in Beth's mind like butterflies caught in a strong wind, but she couldn't think of anything to say.

Weber said, "I'm sure that's why Anderson mentioned her name, Must've been missing his mother, that's all. I wouldn't think about it too hard. Just goes to show you how nuts this guy was."

Something inside Beth fundamentally disagreed with Weber. Someone had missed something. It was all there but no one was putting the information together correctly.

"How did he avoid getting caught for the last four years?" she asked. "And why would he suddenly decide to have a breakdown now? And what did I have to do with any of this? And how did he know my name, and my boyfriend's name?"

"We're still trying to figure all that out, and I assure you we will. It just might take a while."

"But he said he knew me, and I—" Beth didn't know how to say it without sounding crazy, so she just blurted it out. "I believed him when he said he knew me. He wasn't lying."

"You can find out a lot about people by using the internet. I'm sure he was just some creep."

Weber wasn't listening.

Beth wanted to scream.

"Is there anything else?" she asked, struggling to keep her voice level.

Silence on the other end of the phone.

"There is certain information I've been instructed to keep quiet about."

Beth said, "Please. I have to know. It's killing me."

She waited.

"It's his car. Anderson's car. All the paperwork is… *wrong*. The registration is the wrong typeset and it's signed by someone who has never worked at the county clerk's office." It sounded like Weber lit a cigarette. "And the license plate. It's a design that never got past the early stages—a prototype. It shouldn't exist and Anderson shouldn't even know about it. And that dead family of his—their fingerprints are all over that car like they rode in it yesterday. And the money in his wallet…" Weber took a long drag and exhaled.

"What?" Beth asked. "What about it?"

"It's blue. Blue bills. Not green. Saw it myself. And

none of the serial numbers match up. I've never seen anything like it."

There was electricity flowing through Beth's veins. She didn't know what all of it meant, but it had to mean something.

"Forget I said anything," Weber said. "They could fire me."

"Sure," Beth said, her mind racing.

After they hung up, Beth sat down and thought about what Weber had said for a long time. She heard from Detective Weber a few more times in the following months, but he never had the answers he'd promised. Beth began to feel like she had failed David Anderson somehow, like it was her fault that he had died.

He became all she thought about.

She couldn't get the image of him sitting at table twelve out of her mind.

***

Regina liked working at the nursing home. The smell didn't bother her like it did some people. The pay was pretty good. Most of the residents were easy to get along with, and some had become like family to her.

Mr. Robert Evans loved to talk about the war. His body was feeble and failing, but his mind was still sharp. He could recall in detail everything that had happened during his years in the service; listening to his stories was like going back in time.

Mrs. Karen Walters was almost like a grandmother to Regina. She was the nicest person—during the day. At night, the little old lady transformed into a howling demon with the strength of three grown men.

But some residents refused to warm up to Regina, even though she had taken care of them for years. Take Ms. Beth Foster for example: the woman was eighty-three, had no family, and never received visitors, yet no matter how hard Regina tried to get to know her, the old lady would not open up.

"Time for your medicine, Ms. Foster," Regina said as she stepped into the room.

Beth was doing the same thing she did everyday: sitting in her wheelchair and staring out the window. The old woman did not react to Regina's words or presence. Regina went to her and tried to hand her a tiny cup of pills, but Beth would not take it.

"Ms. Foster, you know I can't leave until you take your medicine."

It was odd: Beth never refused her medicine. On the contrary, she always seemed in a hurry to take her pills so Regina would leave.

Regina stood there, holding the cup. Ms. Foster sat frozen in her wheelchair, staring outside.

"Do you ever wonder about what could've been?" the old lady asked.

It was the first question Regina could ever remember Ms. Foster asking.

"Sure. I think it's a pretty natural thing for people to do."

The old lady made an agreeable noise then said, "Do you have any regrets?"

After six years together, Regina couldn't believe Ms. Foster finally wanted to talk.

"I try not to. I mean, there are some things I wish I hadn't done, but regrets...no, I have no regrets."

The old woman chuckled then said, "Regrets are all I have."

Regina lowered the pill-cup and sat down on the edge of the nearby bed.

"What exactly do you regret, Ms. Foster?"

The old lady drew a deep breath and let it out slowly.

"When I was younger, I had dreams. I was going

to graduate college. I was going to love my job. I was going to get married. I was going to have kids—a bunch of them, at least five or six." Her gaze was still locked on something outside the window. "But it never happened. None of it. I never did anything with my life."

Regina didn't know what to say. It was heartbreaking for her to realize how alone some people were. Regina had the opposite problem: she was never alone. She had sisters and brothers and nieces and nephews and three children of her own.

"Give me my pills," the old woman said.

Regina handed her the cup and she knocked back the medicine.

"I'm sorry your life didn't go the way you wanted it to, but you're not alone. I'm here. We see each other everyday. And you don't have to be so distant."

A few seconds passed.

Regina had other patients to attend to, but she didn't want to leave Ms. Foster alone after everything she had said.

"I have to go, but I'll come back to check on you later."

The old lady said nothing. She was still staring out the window.

Regina left the room, but turned and took a final look at Beth Foster before she shut the door. She was suddenly overcome with the feeling that Ms. Foster didn't belong in the nursing home, that some strange series of events had led to her being there, that she was supposed to be somewhere else, somewhere far away and doing something different with her life.

She closed the door.

She leaned against the wall and cried.

Nobody came to comfort her.

She had never felt so alone.

Then she went and took care of her other

patients.

The Sonnet the Ghost Wrote on My Mirror While I Showered
Marcus Wahlbring

Can I explain the pain I feel while passing
through simple mists or subtle beams of sunlight?
It's like what potted plants must feel is missing
as they sit pissing from their too-full pots right
into the earth they don't belong to. Now
a storm spins in the windy crater where
my heart used to be, but I don't know how
to slow it down, to curb the pulsing air
I'll never breathe again. I wish wind didn't hurt.
I wish I could speak with the dust my tongue's
    become.
I speak in touch instead, in song, in dirge not worth
    the dirt
they buried me in. I keep to the dry dark, my home.
If these walls weren't the world, if the world weren't
    the moon,
like you, I'd leave this house, with a body that's
    clean.

The Hungry Swamp
Tom Howard

Arlene stood and brushed the dirt from her knees. Since she'd taken this field assignment, she'd been grungier and more tired than she'd been in her life. But she'd developed a respect for the professor and his students excavating the Native American mounds in southern Ohio.

"Anything?" Professor Singer asked after climbing the hill.

"You were right," Arlene said. "Nothing here but dirt."

The hill contained no bones. He'd said the larger mounds had been built for astronomical purposes and not burial sites.

She'd been lucky she'd found two burial sites already. An unclassifiable psychic, her powers were too vague for most clients. Arlene couldn't tell the future, track an aunt's lost brooch, or levitate the smallest rock. She could sense the emotions of a location, especially one used by a lot of people over time. Train stations and airports gave her throbbing headaches; bucolic anthropological sites, not so much.

The professor removed his handkerchief from his back pocket and wiped his brow. He wore a beige shirt suitable for summertime in Ohio and a pair of jeans. The male and female students, digging in sites identified by Arlene, wore similar outfits.

"There's enough work for us today," he said. "We've found pottery shards from the Paleo people."

"Any bones?"

"Yes. Many in the sites you found. I had my doubts about the university hiring a psychic, but it would've taken us much longer to find them on our own."

"What about the swamp?" she asked.

Professor Singer said the forest below them had once been a bog. The dry patch of ground now contained a grove of gnarled pines. It made her queasy looking at it.

"Unlikely. They didn't use mounds to bury their dead, and they didn't use swamps. Are you sensing something?"

"I'm seeing a fog over the area, which usually indicates a graveyard. It's a manifestation of grief. I avoid cemeteries when I can."

"Ghosts?"

She shook her head. "I'm not sure they exist. This fog is different, angry."

"Let's take a look." Professor Singer clambered down the grass-covered hill.

She followed him, digging in her boot heels to slow her descent. Climbing up and down the mounds would probably do wonders for her glutes.

On flat ground, she hesitated before approaching the woods. The sun squatted low on the horizon, and the fog grew thicker and a deeper red. The swirling mist distorted her view of the twisted trees. If a massacre had occurred there, it must have been devastating to remain visible to her after hundreds of years.

"Here?" the professor asked.

"A little farther." Her skin crawled, and she clenched her fists as if she wanted to strike him. Why? Professor Singer had worked hard to make her feel a part of the team.

Her cheeks flushed, and she unclenched her hands. "Stop!"

"Am I in the fog?" He waved his arms about as if hoping to feel something.

"Yes." She reached forward to pull him back, and

her right arm entered the billowing redness. Warm drops peppered her skin. She yanked her arm back.

The professor stared at her. "Are you okay?"

The skin of her arm was dotted with red spots. Blood.

"Here." He wrapped his handkerchief around her arm.

It didn't hurt. "Can you see the blood?" Her psychic manifestations, such as the crimson fog hovering above the ground, weren't usually seen by normals.

"Yes. I'll get the first aid kit."

She unwrapped the handkerchief. "No. I've stopped bleeding. That's never happened before."

Her skin was patterned with red freckles, and her head throbbed. "Professor, something horrible happened here."

"Are we in danger?"

Rage flowed through her—and something else—but none of it directed at her or the anthropologists. "No. The enemies of whoever is buried here are long dead."

"Professor!" Sam, one of the grad students, approached at a run. Sam had the longest arms and legs Arlene had ever seen. He reminded her of a loping giraffe. He stopped to catch his breath. "There's a call for Arlene from her agency. They need to talk to her immediately."

The professor made everyone leave their cellphones in the jeep each morning when they drove in from a nearby motel.

Mrs. Lentz and her Unique Opportunity employment agency found jobs for people with psychic abilities. Arlene, because of her odd talents, didn't have many employment opportunities.

"Thank you," she said. "Are we finished here, Professor?"

"Look at your arm," he said.

The red freckles were dry smears. She hadn't felt any pain because she hadn't been wounded. "It's not my blood," she said. "It came from the fog."

He nodded. "We'll examine the swamp tomorrow."

A black Hummer pulled across the grass, and two men climbed out.

"Great," the professor said. "Just what we need. A visit from John Patrick."

"Who?"

"A real estate developer," he said.

"But this is state land," Arlene said. "Why would a developer be here?"

"The mineral rights remain in private hands. This guy is trying to buy them out from under us. If he succeeds, we must stop digging."

He walked to meet the men. "Mr. Patrick, I didn't expect to see you here again."

The tall man in a tailored suit smiled. "My lawyers say we're close to securing the rights. Less than seventy-two hours. The university hasn't told you?"

"No. Is that why you came?"

"No, I wanted to meet a real-life psychic. I hear Miss Court is helping you look for Indian bones." Mr. Patrick stepped forward and stuck out his hand at Arlene. "Hello, pleased to meet you."

Unsure of what to say, Arlene shook the developer's hand.

The man gripped her hand too long. "You don't read minds, do you? Meeting a pretty girl could be embarrassing."

She pulled back her hand. "No, I don't read minds." She turned to the professor. "I better take that call."

"I'll return when the contract is signed," Mr. Patrick said. Nodding at the professor and Arlene, he turned and walked to the Hummer.

His fancy boots left deep imprints in the soft ground, but that's not what drew Arlene's attention. His footprints filled with blood as he walked away. She'd never seen land react that way. From the professor's scowl at the departing Hummer, he didn't see the blood.

Keira, another grad student, waited at the Jeep and handed Arlene her phone.

"Mrs. Lentz, is everything okay?" Arlene asked.

The voice at the other end sounded crisp and authoritative, typical for Mrs. Lentz. "Yes, everything's fine. We've got another job for you. Pays well, and the employer insists you start tomorrow. He's bought a tract of land in Canada and would like you to verify it's safe to be occupied."

"What?" If anyone knew her shortcomings, it was Mrs. Lentz. Unless the previous owner had interred dead bodies, Arlene couldn't help. "I can't leave in the middle of an assignment. We're finding strange things here." Bloody swampy things.

A lengthy pause greeted her statement. "You're always finding strange things, Miss Court. I'll ask the university for a leave of absence for you. The new client says it's an emergency."

"Let me discuss it with the professor tonight," Arlene said. "Who is the client?"

Papers shuffled. "JRP Developers. I don't know how they heard about you, but they're determined to hire you."

"I'll let you know in the morning," Arlene said and hung up. She hated turning down an assignment since they seldom occurred, but the swamp worried her.

"Trouble?" Professor Singer asked when he joined her.

"No. What about you? Can Mr. Patrick shut you

down?"

"Don't worry about him." He loaded tools into the back of the Jeep. "Unless he offers a hundred times the assayer's estimate, I doubt the original owners will sell him the mineral rights. Strange that he came out here just to threaten us. Again."

She needed to tell the professor about the bloody footprints. "Professor, could we have a drink after dinner to discuss a few things?"

He smiled. "Only if you call me Roger. I've got a bottle of excellent scotch in my room."

"Sounds good," she said. He probably thought she'd asked him for a date. She had considered it, but she had a boyfriend in New York. They had an off-again, on-again relationship that was currently on-again.

***

"How much do you know about psychics?" she asked across the small table. She hadn't joined him for drinks in his motel room before. She usually had dinner with the group at the diner adjoining the motel.

He lifted his plastic cup to sip 100 Pipers scotch. "When they stuck you on my team, I mean offered your services, I didn't believe in things I couldn't quantify. I looked up psychometry, but you don't quite fit the definition."

"That's the story of my life," Arlene said. "I never fit any definition. Psychometry is determining the history of objects. I can't tell you where this cup has been."

"You can only determine the history of places? Can you tell something about this motel?"

"Not the history. Just the emotions left behind by the people who lived there." She closed her eyes and took a deep breath. "I feel gratitude mostly."

"No lustful rendezvous?"

She laughed. "At a rent-by-the-hour motel, you'd probably be right. But this one is off the beaten path, and tired travelers are glad to find somewhere to stop and rest."

"I see. It would be interesting to run some experiments to see what you can do."

"No thanks. That's how I spent my adolescence," she said. "The university never found a niche for me among the empaths, telepaths, and telekinetics. I learn something new about myself every day." Mostly what she couldn't do.

She told him about the bloody footprints. "I've never seen anything like it. Mr. Patrick may be dangerous if the land reacts so violently to him." She took a sip of the scotch, enjoying the smooth taste and the companionship. She didn't often get that on an assignment.

He leaned back. "The stories about Spotted Horn may be true."

"Who?"

"A legend in the oral record. A fierce chief in this area who led raiding parties that murdered tribes without mercy. We've never found physical evidence he existed. Stories say he sewed up his enemies, still alive, in animal hides and threw them in a swamp to die. The lucky ones drowned. The unfortunate starved or died of dehydration."

"Sounds like a bogeyman story," Arlene said. "Grislier than most. You think this could be the swamp?"

"I don't know. Legends say that with each enemy's death—man, woman, or child—Spotted Horn grew stronger. He could outrun retreating warriors, lift ten men, toss boulders a mile away, and lived twice as long as normal. I guess he had a good publicist."

"Sounds like Mr. Patrick," she said. "The attitude

anyway."

Roger leaned forward. "Are you sure you want to go into that fog again? Let us dig some holes and see what we find."

"When I feel the emotions laid down by people, they're usually temporary. The land wants to return to normal after people leave. But this swamp feels angry and hungry. It's accustomed to death. It craves it."

"You're definitely not going into it again." Roger stood. "Would you like a drink for the road?"

"Very much so, but I need to be clear-headed in the morning. Thanks for listening to me, although it's not the empirical science you're used to."

He shrugged. "I'm all about the learning, Arlene."

She walked to the door, grateful he had an open mind but worried about who or what the swamp hungered for.

***

After a restless night, Arlene grabbed a cup of coffee and met the others in the parking lot.

"You okay?" Roger asked.

She threw her bag in the back. "Do I look that bad?"

"No, I'm worried about you going into that fog."

She'd told Mrs. Lentz she needed to stay a few more days. She suspected JRP Developers belonged to John R. Patrick but didn't understand why he wanted her out of the picture.

"I'll be fine," she told Roger and tried to believe it.

Hours later, exhaustion made her knees wobbly. As a compromise to entering the crimson fog that only she could see, Roger asked her to determine its boundaries. She tied colored flags to trees where the fog reached. No blood covered her, but her being near the insatiable hunger was draining. Plus, the anger made her grumpy. She kept an eye on the anthropologists in the heart of the swamp, but they seemed unaffected.

"Okay," Roger said after she marked the boundary. "We'll chalk a fifty-foot grid and start the dig after lunch."

"I need to sit in a Jeep for a while," Arlene said. "I'm worn out." And getting crankier the longer she spent near the fog. She might strangle someone with the bright yellow cordon tape if they looked at her wrong.

"How about I have Keira take you back to the motel for a nap?" he asked.

"Are you sure?" Arlene sagged against the Jeep. "I'm supposed to help, not be a nuisance."

Roger waved his hand at the fluttering flags. "You've done your share today. Go."

"Thanks." Mr. Patrick's mention of a three-day deadline nagged at her. The motel had a sporadic internet connection, but she might find something online. If not, a nap sounded great.

Keira agreed to run Arlene back to the motel, saying they never found anything interesting on the top layer anyway.

The county road back to the motel wound through the state park. Keira, never chatty, remained silent during the half-hour ride. Arlene appreciated it.

"What the hell?" Keira stared in the rearview mirror.

Arlene turned in her seat. "What it is?"

"Some asshole is riding my ass. I'm going as fast as I can. Hold on. He's coming around."

The road was too narrow for a car to overtake them. As it drew up alongside, it slowed.

"Watch out!" Arlene shouted.

The Mustang smashed into the side of their Jeep and shoved them off the road. Keira fought the wheel, but they skidded into a ditch. Impacting nose-first, their seatbelts and inflated airbags stopped them from crashing through the windshield. The Mustang sped away.

"Are you all right?" Keira beat her airbag aside.

Arlene nodded. "I think so. You?"

"I'll have bruises tomorrow, but I'm okay." She pulled out her phone and called 911, then the professor to tell him what had happened.

They waited for the sheriff to arrive as steam billowed from the busted radiator. A tall man in a big hat, the sheriff stood at the side of the road and shook his head. "What happened? Hit a deer?"

"No," Arlene said. "Someone ran us off the road."

The sheriff frowned. "Are you sure?"

"See that white streak of paint down the passenger side?" Arlene asked. "That wasn't there this morning. A white '73 Mach One Mustang with a black stripe down the hood. Tinted windows. Can't be too many of those around."

"You sure of the year and model?" he asked.

"My boyfriend's a New York cop who takes me to car shows," Arlene said. Let the sheriff think she owed her ability to recognize cars to her boyfriend. It would be quicker than convincing him she knew old cars.

"Yeah," the sheriff said. "Shouldn't be hard. You didn't get the license plate number?" He scribbled in his notebook.

"It didn't have a plate," Arlene said. "Not the smartest criminals around. One of the most recognizable cars in the world, and they removed their license plates."

"True," he said.

Roger arrived and listened to them tell their story again. They called for a tow truck, and Keira offered to wait for it. The sheriff left after Keira signed the accident report.

"Come on," Roger said. "I'll take you to the motel and come back for Keira."

Arlene climbed into the Jeep. "Someone is watching us."

Roger drove in silence for a moment. "That's the psychic talking?"

"No. But they wanted to threaten either Keira or me, and I'm guessing it's me. They had to be watching to send that Mustang. First, they tried to pull me away on another assignment. Then, run us off the road. What the hell is going on, and what are they afraid I'll find?"

"Maybe Mr. Patrick wants to shut us down," Roger said.

"Or he's heard about Spotted Horn and knows the swamp is important."

Roger pulled into the motel parking lot. "Will you be okay here by yourself?"

"Yes. It's only for a couple of hours. People are in and out of the motel all the time, and I'll call the sheriff if anyone tries to break in. Wake me when you get back."

***

Joining the others at the diner when they finished for the day, she took the open seat beside Roger. "Find anything?"

"Too much," he said. "Mr. Patrick will never be able to take this away from us. You're right, it's huge."

His words did not match his sad expression. All the students looked glum as they pushed the meatloaf special around their plates.

"What did you find?" she asked.

"Shrouds," he said. "The swamp mud prevented the animal hides from completely decaying, and the bones are well-preserved."

"Too well preserved," Keira said. "We found

toothmarks on the skeletons. It looked as if people tried to eat themselves rather than starve."

Roger nodded. "Some of them were children. Spotted Horn was a bastard."

No one commented further as they picked at their food.

"I found Mr. Patrick online," Arlene said. Not hungry, she waived the waitress away. "He's got his fingers in a little of everything, land, finances, artifacts."

"Artifacts?" Roger asked. "So, he may have heard about Spotted Horn and the swamp. We've found only bones and animal skins so far. What is he looking for?"

Arlene feared she knew. "According to Google, he's also heavily into arcane sciences."

Keira looked up from her untouched plate. "There's an oxymoron. Like séances and zombies?"

"More like enriching his personal wealth and well-being," Arlene said. "He has a dozen spiritual advisors. He probably believes the stories about Spotted Horn."

"Idiot," Roger said.

Arlene agreed. "How is everyone? Did anyone feel angry or nervous while working in the swamp?"

Everyone shook their heads. Non-psychics hadn't been affected.

"I may know why the seventy-two hours is important," Arlene said. "Tomorrow night is something called a Blood Moon, a full eclipse. It's rare and popular with the supernatural crowd."

Roger pushed his plate away. "So, if Mr. Patrick thinks he has a way to duplicate Spotted Horn's powers, tomorrow night would be the perfect time."

"Not very scientific," Arlene said, "but Mr. Patrick doesn't seem to be a man deterred by facts. What should we do?"

"I'm going to tell the university what we found. We'll set up a rotation to keep an eye on the site for trespassers or unusual activity. Any suggestions? This is more your field than mine."

She shook her head. "No. All I feel from the swamp is hunger and anger. It wants death to return. Again, not scientific but that's what I'm getting."

"I'll make up a roster for tonight's watches," he said. "We'll dig tomorrow until dark."

Arlene didn't look forward to returning to the site, but she couldn't sit at the motel all day waiting for the guillotine to drop.

***

The next day, students cataged the bones and laid them on tables they'd set up in the swamp. Arlene searched the surrounding mounds but found nothing of interest. At lunchtime, she helped by setting out the noon meal in the back of one of the Jeeps.

"Anything new?" she asked Roger when he joined her.

He shook his head. "More of the same. It'll take us months to unearth all the skeletons. You?"

"I'm confused. The swamp is waiting for something but isn't affected by you or your digging. What does it want?"

"Maybe it's only satisfied when someone dies."

She nodded. "Possible. Let's not test it. Something horrible is coming."

"Are you a precog now?" Roger asked with a smile.

"I wish. You've got the wrong psychic for this job." As usual, she was a round peg in a square hole.

He reached for a sandwich. "I'm feeling uneasy, too. It's as if the swamp is one big shroud, capturing the poor souls killed by Spotted Horn."

"Not very scientific, Professor, but well said."

After lunch, she cleaned up while they returned to work. Bundling the trash, she put it in a Jeep. One minute, she lifted a black plastic bag, the next, her head exploded.

***

She awoke with someone breaking rocks inside her skull. She lay on the ground with her hands and feet tied. "What the hell?"

"Ah, Miss Court." Mr. Patrick squatted next to her. "So nice to see you're still with us."

The long shadows revealed the sun had dropped behind the trees while she'd been out. Men she didn't recognize moved in the twilight.

"What's happening?" she asked. "Where are the others?"

"Already in position," he said. "We're just waiting for the blood moon to rise so you can do your part."

Two large men grabbed her and lifted her to her feet. Her head swam. Was she concussed?

"Me?" she asked. "I don't have a part. You tried to get me reassigned, and when that didn't work, you attempted to scare me off. What do you want? If you're looking for gold or tomorrow's winning lottery numbers, you've got the wrong girl."

He brushed dirt and pine needles from her clothing. "I apologize, Miss Court. I didn't realize your role in all this. My advisors say you are important."

She shook her head and regretted it. "Where are the students?"

He pointed to the swamp. "They have a part to play, too."

In the twilight and through the fog, dark lumps lay scattered throughout the forest. Some of them moved.

"No! You can't!" She struggled in her restraints and would have toppled over if not for the guards on either side. "You're insane. You're not Spotted Horn.

You're going to spend the rest of your natural life in prison if you hurt those kids."

Mr. Patrick laughed and pulled out a long knife. "Natural life? After tonight, mine will become considerably longer. Yours, however, will not. According to legend, the shaman needs to be bloodied before the ritual."

The guards turned Arlene with her back to the madman.

"What are you doing?" she asked.

Mr. Patrick moved closer. "Either you'll connect me with the shrouds or you'll die from blood loss." With that, he used the knife to slice twice down Arlene's back through cloth and skin. She screamed from the scalding pain, and the men dragged her to the edge of the fog as the sun disappeared. They cut her ties and pushed her past the colored flags.

Blinded by the fog and quickly covered by patches of blood—some her own—she stumbled forward. The fog's hunger hit her like a physical blow.

She wiped fog droplets from her forehead. The haze fogged her vision. Her back stung when blood from the fog mingled with hers, and the bump on the back of her head pounded.

She tripped over a writhing sack. She groped in the dirt for a stick or a stone. Although Mr. Patrick and his men weren't blinded by the fog, she hoped they couldn't see her in the twilight. She found a piece of flint with a sharp edge and located the thongs knitting the cowhide together. Sawing quickly before Mr. Patrick saw what she attempted or turned on a light, she cut a small slit.

The person inside wiggled, and she put her mouth close to the opening. "It's me, Arlene. Use this stone to cut yourself free but don't jump out. Crawl close enough to someone else to free them."

"Arlene?" She recognized Sam's voice. "What are

you going to do?"

Mr. Patrick and his men huddled at the edge of the swamp. The fog seemed thicker toward them. They seemed afraid to enter the swamp.

"They wanted a ritual," she said. "I'm going to give them one. I'll distract them while you free the others."

She stood, whooped, and waved her arms in the air. She supposed she looked a sight covered with blood.

Spinning, she stamped her feet and shouted nonsense syllables. She stomped to the edge furthest away from her captors. Two men ran around the swamp to intercept her. The fog thinned the farther she traveled from Mr. Patrick. When she ran in another direction, the men moved to stop her but didn't enter the swamp.

She stumbled, weakening while the swamp's hunger grew. Tripping over a cowhide, she found it empty. Sam had freed some of the others.

The fresh cowhide deposited more blood on her. She'd been smeared with blood from the fog, her wounds, and now butchered cows. She probably looked like Carrie at the prom.

"What's the plan, Arlene?" Roger crawled on his elbows and knees to where she lay panting on her stomach.

"I don't know. Patrick thinks I can bind him and the swamp together, but I can't." Her head swam, and darkness closed around her.

Roger shook her awake. "At least they're not shooting at us. You said none of this made sense. Is the swamp still hungry?"

The Blood Moon climbed the sky. The fog thinned in the forest. Only Mr. Patrick's area remained enshrouded and fuzzy.

"He needs the swamp to kill us." Arlene's back stung. "But the swamp doesn't want us. It wants the man who created it." The surrounding fog had cleared so much that no blood dripped on Arlene, but her back hurt, and she could barely raise her head.

"But Mr. Patrick isn't Spotted Horn," Roger said.

"No, but he's so soulless the swamp thinks he is. Part of the ritual must have been for Spotted Horn to return to the swamp when he died. He didn't, and the swamp has been waiting for him for centuries."

"How do we give it what it wants?"

"We help the swamp. Find some bones."

"What about you?"

"I'll just lie here until Mom calls me down to breakfast." A short nap would be nice.

Roger shook his head and crawled away. He returned with an armful of bones from the pits they had dug.

"Throw them at Mr. Patrick." She could barely hear herself speak, but she gathered what little strength she had and dug her fingers into the soil. She inhaled the fog and blew it in Mr. Patrick's direction. "We'll extend the swamp to him."

Roger hurled the bones toward Mr. Patrick. She gathered the fog into herself and expelled it toward him. The Blood Moon turned scarlet as the eclipse progressed. The fog rushed at him as if a dam had burst. Mr. Patrick staggered, shouting at his men. His orders stopped as he choked on the fog.

The fog wrapped him tightly, but instead of covering him in the blood of long-dead victims, it leeched blood from him and tore holes in his flesh. Fog poured out the holes, and flesh left his skeleton.

Arlene passed out as Mr. Patrick's bloody skeleton collapsed, hoping her mom wouldn't yell at her for falling back asleep on a school day.

***

She lay on her stomach in a hospital bed. Too often, she found herself in a hospital following an assignment.

Moaning, she tried to turn over.

"Don't." Roger rose from his chair beside her. "You've got stitches and a concussion. They had to transfuse you. You probably won't be able to lie on your back for a while."

"What happened? Is everyone okay?"

He returned to his seat. "Everyone is fine. Except for Mr. Patrick, and all that's left of him is a pile of bones. His goons ran off when he died."

"Pile of bones?"

"I wouldn't testify to it, but your theory about the swamp waiting all these years for someone like him may be the correct hypothesis."

The hungry swamp had been sated at last. "This would have been over a lot sooner if I'd pushed him into the swamp that first day," she said. It would be much easier when places learned to talk and tell her what they wanted.

"How long until I'm back on my feet?" she asked.

"Are you in a hurry to return to work?"

The fog and hunger had likely vanished from the site, but she wanted to see for herself. "Like the swamp, I can't leave a job unfinished."

"It's not going anywhere," Roger said. "Get some rest."

She did feel a little fuzzy from the meds. "Tell Mom I feel too sick to go to school today."

Evening in the Infirmary
Rob E. Boley

A river rages under the house.

The night has consumed the moon
leaving only starlight cookie crumbs.

In places meant for dreams, we instead
offer space for the long dead who suffered
by hook and bar, by ten rules, by endless toil.

In the field out back, these upright citizens lost
even their names to the grind of the shadows that
flicker on the walls, stagnate behind doors, and nest
in the ceilings while the occasional stair goes
nowhere.

"Nature's Horns" by Sonali Roy

Blood Beach
Gregory Jeffers

The ferry I'd barely managed to catch landed at the Vieques pier at 10:10 Sunday morning. The rub rails lamented against creosoted dock pilings reawakening the self-pity I had conjured up for this mission. The few fishermen still at work tied up and off-loaded their meager catches. Gulls hovered over the disappearing wake of the ferry, hunting churn-ups. The pilot revved the engine in reverse to slow our entry and black diesel puffs billowed above the exhaust stacks like artificial clouds in a Lon Chaney movie.

The island looked much the same as when Mom and I had left three years earlier. More plastic litter, maybe. A few more stray cats. Definitely more chickens patrolling the dirt sidewalks prowling for cockroaches or centipedes.

I had no idea where Dad might be, so headed to my Uncle Diego's rooms above the Viejo Sombrero Bar.

I knocked. A minute later, he pulled the door open cautiously. He blinked three times and rubbed at the grey stubble on his chin with the back of his hand.

"Mateo?" His eyes brightened. "Mateo. Come in boy."

I entered, and he hugged me, then patted me on the back and finished with a soft punch to my shoulder. "Eh, but not a boy any longer. I hear you got yourself a scholarship to university. Always knew you were the smart one. Smartest kid in Vieques." He exaggerated, but I had been the tall, skinny kid who was mocked for actually going to school every day and studying at night.

"You want coffee?"

"No, thanks. I don't have a lot of time. I'm trying to find Dad. Do you know where he is living?"

Diego pursed his thin lips and snatched a pack of Lucky Strikes off the kitchen table behind him. "I can tell you where he is living, but he's not at home. He's in jail."

"Jail? Shit. What'd he do?"

"Sit down."

I did.

His apartment was small and sparsely furnished. Smelled of lemon furniture polish and ivory soap. It was tidy in a comfortable way.

"He's doing six months for putting out a man's eye in a brawl at the Plaza Bar." He jammed a cigarette between his lips and lit it with a stick match. "We were shooting pool with two marines from the base. One guy, big one with a shaved head, scratched on a bank shot at the eight ball.

When your dad fetched a stripe out of the corner pocket to set for the scratch, the guy laid the tip of his cue over your dad's hand. 'What are you doing?' he asked in a nasty tone.

" 'Setting for your scratch.'

" 'Weren't no scratch.' Man had a Mississippi or Alabama drawl. People from all those states sound the same to me and, I believe, to your Dad.

"The bar went silent. Your dad set the ball gentle as an egg at the rack dot.

"Guy goes, 'Said it wasn't a scratch. I ticked the ten ball.'

"Your dad smiled a friendly smile. 'Don't think so, Amigo. Ten ball hasn't budged a pubic hair.'

"I guess that's all it took. Well, that, a twenty dollar wager, and sixteen shots of Bacardi split between two Puerto Ricans and two young Marines. Your dad was getting the crap choked out of him by

54

the big guy. He lifted his cue up straight as a missile and caught the guy in the eye." Diego exhaled a long plume of smoke through his nose. "Game over."

"Sounds like self-defense to me."

"If it'd been another Viequense who lost his eye, the judge might have seen it that way. But it was a U.S. Marine. Lucky it didn't happen on the base. Your Dad's a naval base guard. He would be doing five to ten years if there'd been a court-marshal."

"You been over to see him?"

"I know I should. Sorry, Mateo. But, you know, the jail is attached to the slaughterhouse. The smell is bad enough, but these last two years been some real bad juju."

"Witchcraft?"

"Haunted."

***

I hoofed it over to the jail at the northern end of the island. The beach there was named Playa de Sangre—Blood Beach—because the offal, bones, skin and blood from the slaughterhouse were washed across the street and into the ocean every afternoon. Blood Beach. Should have been Blood and Guts Beach.

I arrived hot and sweaty. A guard slouched in front of the steel gate of a roofless courtyard that adjoined the slaughterhouse. Not much of a guard really. Tattered tee shirt, baggy-ass jeans and no weapon. Big guy. A cratered complexion indicated he'd been through some nasty pox or another. The face of a burro, flat yellow teeth the size of hotel soap. The stench from the slaughterhouse next door was overwhelming. I fought back a gag instinct and caught the guards eye.

I nodded toward the cells. "Ricardo Santana," I said, referring to my father.

"Who are you?"

"Mateo Santana Lopez. His son."

He opened the gate. "Number three."

He didn't need to bother. The eight cells stretched along the courtyard where it abutted the slaughterhouse. It wouldn't be hard to pick out my father. I hadn't seen him since I was fourteen, but there'd be no missing that scar. Ran from just under his right eye damn near to his chin. Been there longer than I'd been alive.

Candy wrappers, flip top cigarette boxes and disposable diapers littered the busted brick floor, tumbling around in the hot wind like leaves do in nicer places. The dog shit stayed put. Two cats quarreled over a tin can in the corner, yowling like possessed banshees. I shuffled over to number three, cell the size of a casket.

"Dad?"

He looked up, squinted, then gaped. "Mateo? Jesu, what are you doing here?"

"Mom sent me."

That shut him up, but he continued to stare at me. The stubble on his face was about half an inch long, and he was thinner than I remembered. Jail does that to you, I guess, especially one next to a slaughterhouse

"She needs you to come home. Nothing permanent. Just a visit."

"For what?"

"She's got pancreatic cancer. Going fast." I developed a momentary tic.

He winced.

"She wants to see if you can forgive her."

He stared at the dirt floor, then back at me. "If I do, will *you* forgive *me*?"

"Not sure. I'll have to wait and see if she forgives me after you forgive her."

More of the shut up.

"I'm only about a month into this six-month stint."

"What about bail?"

"Bail? This is Vieques, Mateo. There's probably not two hundred dollars in hard currency on the whole fucking island."

A gust of wind sent a Campbell's tomato soup can rolling in front of me. I kicked it toward the cats. "I'll talk to the jailor. Where is he?"

Dad gazed at the back wall of his cell adjoining the slaughterhouse. "He owns the butchery. Office is upstairs. Probably not up there unless he's still entertaining from last night. Don't expect any favors from him. He's got a contract with the mayor to run the jail and is interested in only one thing." He lifted his hand and rubbed the first two fingers against his thumb. "Name is Johnny Drip."

"What the hell kind of name is Drip?"

"Gringo. Texas, I think."

"I'll find him. If I don't get back today, I'll come by in the morning."

"Don't come at night."

"I wasn't planning on it, but why?"

He gazed to the back wall of his cell. "Noises." The he turned to me and shrugged. "Just noises."

"Yeah, so I'll either be back this afternoon or tomorrow morning."

"Won't be here after seven in the morning. I'll be working."

"Working?"

"Yeah. We all work in the slaughterhouse. Part of our sentencing." He pulled his shoulders back and grinned. "I'm a butcher now."

"Who came up with that idea? Satan?"

"The judge." He paused. "In Vieques the mayor is also the judge."

***

The slaughterhouse door was locked, but sounds drifting from the second floor windows—four or five meters above street level due to the high ceilings on the first floor—indicated people upstairs were waking from a tequila induced siesta and playing around with the idea of some carnal entertainment to work off the hangover. Just my imagination, of course, but didn't prove to be too far from the truth. The usual guttural undertones with lingering ess and cha sounds; some light slaps; lamenting bed springs; swishing of bed linens too sweaty and crumpled to rustle; clinking of a bottle neck on glass rims; flinting of a Zippo; burning stale tobacco, a few feminine sobs, then the low cajoling voice of a man with a desperate need and sudden manners.

I walked around the outside and at the opposite corner stood on the hood of a fenderless dilapidated jeep to look through one of the barred window openings into the slaughterhouse. The putrid smell of unattended death floated into my face. A decade of accumulated animal grease drip-trailed the plank walls, and the floors had the sheen of liquid lard. I jumped down and blew hard through my nose.

I figured if I waited outside long enough Drip's woman would leave to return to whatever she called home and I would get my talk with Johnny Drip. It was mid-afternoon when the steel plate door finally groaned open and a short, stocky woman of indeterminate age peered through the opening. I sat across the street on a trash can I had turned upside down, tapping my heels against the galvanized steel in feigned casual indifference, until she wobbled out the door and tottered down the street, leaving the door agape.

I crossed the street.

The guard left his post at the jail gate and intercepted me. "What do you want?"

"I need to talk to Mr. Drip about buying my father's release."

This lightened his taut face noticeably. He told me to wait, went up and a minute later returned to the door and led me upstairs.

By anyone's measure, Drip was a quintessential Texas oil and beef man. The beef was on his belly, the oil on his drawn face. A bulbous nose bullied his cheeks and ferrety chin. What compelled him to expatriate to Vieques was anyone's guess. Probably running from a lawsuit or a woman. But honestly, I didn't give a shit. I just needed to buy Dad's way out of Drip's two-bit jail.

Drip stared at the guard. "You can go, Manny."

"Let me get to the point," I said, offering myself a chair in front of his desk.

"Take a seat," he said magnanimously, although three seconds late. With the tattered and dark-yellowed sleeveless tee shirt he very much resembled a bowling pin meagerly dripped in caramel sauce.

A doorway to my left entered onto what appeared to be a closet with a bed. Ha. Real Romeo, this guy.

"My father is in your pen, and I need to pay his bail. My mother is dying and wants to see him. Simple." I hustled my balls, thinking it might create some low caste comradery. "How much?"

With one finger he scratched the capillary-latticed dimple that was his empurpled cheek. "Bail?"

"Novel approach in this part of the world. But, yes, I'm talking about giving you some money to release my father."

"You want a drink?" He had an annoying way of snuffling that lifted the right side of his upper lip into a curl.

"No."

Sliding a drawer open, he extracted a pint bottle of Bacardi and a glass. Went through the ceremony.

"Five hundred ought to do it."

What? Had I dressed too well? "Five hundred dollars? I don't have that kind of money."

"No rush. Maybe you can raise it. Your mother got some?" He threw back the rum.

"What my mother has is terminal cancer. And six children."

"Any other relatives got some money?"

If this was the guy's way of expressing his sympathy for Mom's condition, it went right over my head. I guess my pondering wasted too much of his time, as he stood and interrupted my brief thoughts.

"Yeah, well, you'll have to leave now cause I got to get to afternoon mass. Let me know when you have the cash and I'll take care of the details." His lips snagged on his teeth as he tried a smile.

"No need to show me out," I said. "Place only has one door."

***

The Meroles family owned the only two supermarkets on the island. Had for generations. I figured if there was any sizable cash sitting around, it would be at their house in Barrio Destino. I had no real plan. Beg? Borrow? Steal? Still, the afternoon was upon me, hot and ponderous, and I had to do something. So I trudged the two miles south to their place.

Sunday afternoon, they'd either be at church or some family barbecue on one of the beaches. No way did I figure them to be at home. So, yeah, right. It was the stealing option that was on my mind. I'd never thieved before except for some penny candy as a kid, then later when I was thirteen as a prank, but this was the most desperate situation I had ever been in. It slowly grew on me that some, if not most, theft has desperate root. Except, of course, for the wealthy suburban klepto housewives and the stylish Riviera diamond thieves who dressed in leotards. But most theft, at least at basic levels, had to do with feelings of fraught need accompanied by wealth inequality that had haunted humankind since the dark ages.

Was I rationalizing? Justifying a crime I was about to commit based on age old social conventions? People have done jail time for this. Some have given their lives for this. Still, I needed to get Dad home.

The gates were locked. Good sign, actually. I scaled the stone wall and dropped into the courtyard. The house was concrete and brick, the roof red clay tile baked light orange by the sun. The gardens were immaculately groomed, the trees pruned in ornamental bobs. Peacocks strutted about a fenced coop and chickens roamed freely. Where were the dogs?

Where were the fucking dogs?

Everyone on Vieques had a dog. Dozen or so rich people had two or three dogs. Here, not a dog in sight. Eerie.

The doors and windows were locked, so I broke a pane in the dining room door with a patio brick, reached in and slid the bolt.

It was one of the most beautiful interiors I had ever seen. The floor was an intricate mosaic of blues and greens, the walls done in an Indian motif of tile wainscoting with hardwood panels above. Brilliant white stucco on the ceiling.

I turned to scan the walls, and as I reached the doorway to my left, my heart stopped. An older woman stood in the frame coddling a wine glass. She was thin but not frail. Grey hair fastened at the top and sides so that it fell about her like fine limbs on a miniature flamboyant. Dressed for a formal dinner. Still her demeanor was casual.

My stare met hers.

She sipped from the glass then returned it to

waist height. "You should not have broken the glass."

I had no response.

"Tell me you are sorry for breaking the glass."

This seemed a good opportunity. "I'm...I'm sorry I broke the glass, Señora."

"What is so urgent that you need to break into my house?"

"I am truly sorry, Señora. I am desperate to get my father out of jail. My mother is dying and wants to see him."

She picked a wisp off her cheek and tucked behind an ear. "Ah. I remember. You are one of the Sanchez boys aren't you?" She leaned against the door jamb. "Ricardo and Isabella's son. Your father is at Blood Beach for putting out a Marine's eye."

"It was a fight," I said, elevating my voice so that it set her back on her heels a bit. I stammered on in a quieter voice. "It was a fight."

"I know, child. Poor choice of someone to fight with. Battle the conquerors, you will be viewed as rebellious. Bolivar said that, I think. Would you like a glass of wine?"

"I don't drink."

"We all start sooner or later. It is only the matter of when one stops that is of importance. It is usually a life altering event. And most often, death is when we stop." She sipped again. "But back to your desperate situation, young man. What is it exactly, and how can I help? And please, for God's sake, what is your first name?"

"I am Mateo, Señora. I need five hundred dollars to bribe Jonny Drip to let my father escape."

She entered the room and set her glass on the credenza. "So you break into my house to steal money? Not very sporting." She strode the three steps to the rear patio door and drew back the curtains. Three of the largest pit bulls I have ever seen sat outside the glass. One cocked its head to observe me. The other two instantly started snarling.

"How curious. They seem to want to come in. Odd. They've already been fed. Shall I let them in?"

"No. I'll leave."

"Oh, no, please. I must insist you stay." She closed the blinds then lifted her glass, sipped, and placed it back down with the gentleness and thoughtfulness one might tender a one-winged pet canary, continuing to stare at it, apparently lost in thought. Finally she turned to me.

"You only have to promise to pay me back."

"What?"

"I will lend you the five hundred. Any boy who would do this for his mother I trust to keep his word. But you have to pay me back. I only hope you are able to do it while I am still alive, so that I can relish my good instincts. Wait here."

I took those moments she was gone to look around. I did not at that time know anything about art, but even a fool could tell the massive paintings were original, laying back modestly in heavily brocaded and gilt frames. And the sculptures, though small, were stone or bronze and meticulously realistic.

She returned and held out a neat stack of twenties.

I reached for it.

"First, you must promise."

I stared at her for a long moment. "I promise to pay you back, Señora." Remarkably, tears welled in my eyes. I took the money. "I cannot express my gratitude sufficiently."

"Wipe your eyes, child. Life is full of lessons if we are only willing to face them. Now you must go. The dogs will be getting jealous." She smiled, a toothless, yet mirthful smile. "And Rosalie has my dinner ready.

I'd invite you to stay, but she is such a terrible gossip everyone on the island would have us in bed together by morning."

She led me to the door and touched an edge of the broken glass. "Next time, please use the knocker." She opened the door. "One more thing. Stay away from the slaughterhouse. It is haunted."

She looked much too intelligent to believe in hauntings. I raised my eyebrows.

"Drip let an old prisoner die in the slaughterhouse. Story goes the prisoner cut off his hand in the bandsaw working a late night shift on his own. Drip let him die rather than risking a run in with the authorities from San Juan. Others say the real reason was something personal between Drip and the old man. He—the old prisoner—was a familiar local sight and a bit loco."

"What was he in jail for?"

"Arson. The old guy liked to watch things burn. Never hurt anyone. Always torched old unused buildings, mostly on the abandoned sugar plantations."

"Why didn't anyone prosecute Drip."

"No corpse."

"Wow."

"It gets worse. Some folks say the old guy ended up in the hamburger. But it's all legend." She opened the door.

I stared into her eyes for the last time, admiring her grace. "Why are you doing this?"

"I had a son once. But that is another story." She ushered me out with a shallow sweep of her hand. "I look forward to your return, Mateo."

Four months later, the true—or additional—reason for her kindness would be revealed when she died of lung cancer.

***

I was barely out of Destino when three banditos mugged me and took the money. One was Drip's personal guard, Manny, who made no attempt whatever at disguise. I fought back but was no match for any one of these desperate men. The second time they knocked me down, I stayed there. They left.

My thoughts were clouded by depression and an overpowering new malaise about injustice at every level, a topic I had not yet dwelled on in my young adulthood. Fortunately, the robbers had not taken my backpack. They knew what they were looking for and had no use for any additional baggage. I pulled out the sandwich I had made the night before and ate it slowly, still sitting where I'd last been laid out.

I decided to spend the night on Blood Beach in order to approach Drip as soon as he arrived, hoping I could convince him to let my father go.

I built a driftwood fire and roasted breadfruit on a stick. As I bit into the first slice a man approached in the wavering light of the fire.

"Who is it?" I called in a tremulous voice.

"No need to be afraid, son. Just a poor beach bum who would enjoy a few moments at your fire." He came closer. Even in the flared light of the flames, his face was wan as a Chinaman's. He was thin as a scepter but carried himself well, almost as if he floated. The eyes of one who has, perhaps, seen too much. Watery, grey, and incredulous. "Name is Luis Torrent."

"I'm Mateo Sanchez. Come sit if you like. Are you hungry? I have smoked breadfruit."

"Very kind, but I've little appetite." He sat on one of the large drift wood chunks I'd hauled close to the fire. "But I will warm myself if I may."

I thought it odd he could have a chill on a seventy-five degree evening, but he was very thin, so I held my tongue.

"I've always enjoyed a good fire," he said, rubbing one hand on a knee. "What brings you here, son?"

I told him.

"Mm. Sad story so far. What will you do now?"

"I will speak to Johnny Drip again. See if I can convince him."

"You do realize there is no way to gain an empathetic ear with that dog?"

"I suppose so, but I don't know what else to do."

"The keys to the cells hang under his desk, where the chair slides in. Why not break in and steal them?"

I was shocked and excited at the same time. "The slaughterhouse is haunted, I hear. And the steel door is locked. I could not break in."

"Don't go through the slaughterhouse. The window above is not locked. No bars, either."

"But it is fourteen feet above the street."

"The wall is stone. You can scale it."

"I don't know."

"Sleep on it for an hour or two. But don't waste the cover of darkness." Then he stood and disappeared into the night.

***

I must have slept for at least two hours because when I woke the crescent moon was lofted directly overhead, the night sky full of stars.

I got on my feet and skulked around the slaughterhouse, perusing the situation. A wind had picked up. No lights were on. Not a sound except the whistle of wind on the jail bars and snoring from the cell yard.

The wall below the window looked climbable. Stones stuck out at various depths and angles offering hand holds and foot rests. I started up slowly, but it proved to be not much of a task. Within a minute, I was at the office window. It was shuttered with a pair of old wood ventanas. I pushed, and they swung in with a groan. Moonlight washed across the floor to the desk. Empty.

I pulled myself up, swung both legs over the windowsill, and dropped quietly to the floor. I tiptoed across the room and, as Luis had reported, the keys hung on a ring under Drip's desk.

No sooner had I grabbed them when the interior door slammed behind me. I froze, listening. Heavy breathing forced me to turn around.

It was Manny, the largest meat cleaver I have ever seen, nearly as long as his leg, hanging from his hand. He tossed handcuffs onto the desk. "Put 'em on."

I stared at them.

He cocked his wrist, bringing the cleaver parallel to the floor and pointed at my stomach. *Shit. Now I'm going to end up in one of those filthy cells.* I dropped the ring of keys and ratcheted the cuffs around my wrists.

"Downstairs," he said, waving the blade toward the door.

At the bottom of the stairs, I reached for the bolt on the exterior door.

"No. The other one."

"The other what?"

"The other door."

"Into the slaughterhouse?" I eyed him briefly.

"Do it."

I opened the door. The stench was overwhelming. No amount of lye could have taken the butchery out of that huge room. He shoved me in and flipped on a switch. Three rows of dusty incandescent bulbs glowed yellow, adding more shadows than illumination. On my right, six beef or horse carcasses hung from hooks, still bleeding out. Two trolley vats of defrocked chickens sat on my left, iridescent flies working them in a buzzing fury. A couple of partially rendered goats lay on a block table. Three legs of something stuck upright out of a grinder the size of a plaza statue.

"Over there," Manny growled, pointing to the far corner with the machete. "The band saw." It was enormous, floor to ceiling, the two-inch blade glinting dully.

I did not like where this was headed but saw no good options. I slouched to the saw and he pinned me into the corner with the blade and toggled the band saw switch. It came on with a rattle and gained speed until it was whirring like a helicopter.

"Your hands," he said.

"What? Are you crazy?" I realized fully the seriousness of the matter.

He lifted the blade to his shoulder. "It's your hands or your head," he said, with a toothy grimace.

A pop loud as a .22 caught our attention and the floor lit up in a strip of flame from the opposite corner, racing toward us like a lightning bolt. Manny's pant leg burst into flame. He swatted at it in surprise and anguish. In a second, his clothing was aflame. He stumbled about, smacking his arms and legs. When his hair caught on fire, he stumbled into the saw head first. Red bits of bone and flesh flew across the room, much of it into my face.

By the time I regained my senses, fire was climbing the walls. I squinted through the haze and passed my wrists on each side of the band saw blade. Squealing and sparks finally gave way to a pop and the small chain of the handcuffs split.

Smoke from the suet soaked floorboards and lard impregnated walls billowed above the flames, blinding me, searing my nose and throat. I choked and hacked, stumbling out of the room. I focused on the keys and bounded up the stairs two at a time.

Snatching the ring off the desk, I turned back toward the stairs but the flames had ascended, now a roaring inferno.

It was a fourteen foot drop to the street, but I had no choice. I sprinted for the window and vaulted over the sill. To my utter surprise, I had a soft landing, accompanied by someone's scream. I had landed on Drip, who must have been alerted by the flames. Turned out, he was not only out cold, but dead as well. He had dropped onto the tip of his knife, clenched in his fist. It stuck out of his throat, the hilt dripping in blood.

***

The morning ferry left at eight. I kept my hands in my pockets until we were a few hundred yards off shore, not intending to display my wrist jewelry while within reach of whatever law enforcement might still be in Vieques.

My father stretched both hands over his head and sucked in a deep breath of the brine air. "How did you know where to find the keys?"

"An old man on the beach told me. Said his name was Luis Torrent."

"Luis Torrent? Cannot be."

"What do you mean, Dad?"

A gull landed on the gunwale and eyed us. It took me a second to focus. I'd never seen a bird with only one claw. He seemed to perch just fine.

I turned to my dad and repeated my question. "What do you mean I could not have met Luis Torrent?"

"Luis Torrent was a prisoner at Blood Beach who disappeared three years ago. Suspicious circumstances."

I stared in disbelief. Eels churned in my stomach, but the nausea abated as the gull squawked twice and flapped off. We both turned to watch as it was joined by two others. They disappeared at the horizon, three small, thin-lined vees like in a kid's drawing.

Spring Brings Everything Back to Life
Renee Cronley

I find comfort in the cold spots
emanating from my empty home
after the warmth of my beloved
disappeared beneath a plot of earth
marked with a marble stone.
I can't imagine her lively spirit
contained inside a cedar box.
Memories spill out in the spring
of her bright eyes greeting lilacs
poking out from their buds—
her sing-song voice carolling their praise.
I can still hear her inhaling them—
her delicate, satisfied sighs behind me.
That kind of passion for life can't die.
Maybe that's why she's come back.

Act of Creation
Donna J. W. Munro

Larmer's babe came on the third night of the dark moons, when usually newborn babes are set out for the dead to take.

But she, alone, birthed him in the velvety dark. Her husband Jonahn fallen dead from farming the cliffs this last six months, her grief for him so deep some thought she'd kill herself and the babe before the moons turned their faces back and chased the dead back into the cliff caves to the world of the dead.

We heard her screaming, knew the babe had come, but who would risk the trek in the dead's dark night to her hut and her side? None of us were fools.

When the night passed and the babe lay wrapped safe in her arms, not a sacrifice for the angry dead as the tradition went, she told us, "Once I held him, his eyes met mine and I knew Jonahn's ka had settled in him. How could I put him out in the dark? How could they take him from me twice?"

Even as we shifted foot to foot with worry for the anger of the dead, we understood her pain. We'd all paid the blood price to the dead, either with our babes, our loves, or our elders. But the two of them had been special even among us. Jonahn and Larmer's love had been clasp of iron banded on their souls, a promise they made in the meat of their bones and the heat of their skin. It sang in their love and flowered in Larmer's care for the babe. The magic of such a thing, the elders whispered, might be enough to keep the curse of the hungry dead from her child of Joahn.

But we watched the babe with the knowing eyes. She named him Shine, after the turning moon and loved him knowing that her soul was made whole again in loving Jonahn's ka growing in Shine, twirling with her own as joined souls often do.

But we watched as he grew.

***

"Shine," Larmer called, voice a joyful song as she spoke to him, the heart beating outside her chest, "did you exercise your arms today? Won't be but long until you'll work the cliffs and I won't have you fall like your Da did."

Shine shook his head. Da didn't fall, but ma couldn't know that. He'd been taken by them who knew the future as well as the old knew the past. Pushed by the dead of the caves so that Shine could be born. Twas a bargain struck between the dark and da, his ka spoke to him in stories, a dark moment of truth and trade between worlds.

"Ma, I'll not work the cliffs. I know it. I have other works to do. Other things my ka made for me."

Larmer's smile faltered when he talked like this, voice too deep for an eleven-turn child, thoughts too deep for a cliff farmer. Shine knew it bothered her when her fictions about him cracked. He tried not to linger in the gray of her worry for him.

"I'll work out after we eat," he conceded, though he couldn't make himself sound happy about it.

She sighed into her lump of cliff flour dough and punched frustration into the yellow mash with twisting knuckles. Poor ma wanted to be a normal family, even though she knew it wouldn't happen. The years of watchful neighbors and whispers behind hands strained in the crinkles around her eyes, in the white at her temples.

He was what he was and none of the village's questions or her seeking tradition would make him different.

"You'll be a man this year," she said, smile tight as she pounded the dough with more than a knead.

"You'll climb the cliffs, touch the sea, take a wife..."

"Ma, none will have me."

"Nonsense, boy. Fine young girls are always watching you. I see them when we bring loaves to the square."

He shuffled toward the table and sat on the plain bench he'd made for her when he'd been just four turns. It wobbled under his weight, imperfect but still his creation. Still a thing he'd brought into the world for her. The satisfaction of making sang in his ka each time he formed a thing. It was his true calling to create, but the cliff farmers didn't value such things as much as a strong back and agile feet on a cliff.

"Ma, they watch because I scare them. I'm the only moonless child to be allowed to live. Those girls have had baby brothers and sisters set out for the dead every turn, disappearing in the dark of the moons. They watch me with suspicion. With fear. There's no wife for me. Besides... my soul doesn't long for love. I am satisfied without."

Larmer stopped pounding and looked into his eyes, her gaze full of so many things. A mother's worry for her lonely boy. A wife's relief for the ka of her gone husband still caring for her even in the next life. His lot was too complex to bring another ka in between them. And besides, when he looked at his mother's face, a part of him told him that no other ka would make him happy. That his ka and hers would find each other in another cycle, so this cycle was meant not for love but for work. And his fingers itched with the magic of making.

"I'll find my way, ma. Don't worry," he said and stood, to go and practice his art away from the hut where none might stop him.

"You'll still have to climb, Shine. The cliffs are hard and I won't have them take you."

He thought for a moment about the test that all

twelve turns must complete. That all who'd be grown and full members of the village must climb the cliffs and stare into the caves of the dead. That some fell and some went mad as the dead stared back. The strongest or weakest might fail. Might jump rather than live with what they saw in those caves. Or maybe, like his da, they'd made a deal.

But his ka whispered to him secrets that only Johan could know and he knew the way he'd get past the test. The way he'd win the trial and the respect of the cliff people. He'd win through making. Through the magic he hid within.

***

"The boy takes such care during the slaughters. He is gentle with the meat dogs and the pulley horses past their use. Once the meat is carved, he gathers up the bones and carries them away."

The men stood head-to-head in a circle as the moons rose for the night. Their homes, ringing around the center of the village on the top of the cliff faced inward, though Shine and his Ma lived on the edge and faced the cliff, an out of square tooth in the town's throat.

"It's nothing to us," one of the men said, smoking a cliff flower wrap, clouds of yellow and brown puffing up and around his round, bald head. "He swings the axe true. Keeps his mouth shut. Knows when to step aside for his elders. Larmer raised him respectful."

The others nodded, though one turned toward the off-kilter hut on the edge of the cliff.

"But why does he take the bones?"

They all nodded and watched. Watched as they always did.

***

Larmer wrapped her boy tight in cliff gear, checking the knots as she had for Joahn, as tears rolled silent and fat down her ashy cheeks. Shine stood stiff as she worked, tried not to notice the sobs stifled behind her hand or the terror that tremored in her fumbling fingers.

"Twelve-turns. How could it have come so fast," she said and glanced up at him shyly from the knot she tied on his ankle. She took a deep steadying breath and stood, gaping his shoulders with damp hands. She looked deeply into his eyes, searching for what Shine didn't know.

He just held her eyes. Tried to radiate calm for her, even if his stomach turned.

She didn't know he'd done it. Didn't know that he'd made the greatest thing. And he didn't know what the making meant for him with the cliff farmers, but it felt so right.

They made their way to the square, where the other twelves waited, trussed and ready to climb. They shook out hard muscles and stretched before the others, knowing that they were in the peak of their lives. Knowing they'd never be more important than they were today. The tradition dictated it. And the other farmers and their children too young sang their praises as they did for each twelve ceremony.

Shine took his place next to Jorcer, a black-haired girl who'd never said a word to him in his life. On her other side stood Cleon, a boy who'd thrown stones at Shine when they'd been five or six turns old. Both kept their eyes forward and their chests out, soaking up the song into their muscles and bones for strength.

The songs weren't for Shine and he knew it.

His mother stood at the edge, always alone in the crowd of them. They weren't cruel to her, but just the same they didn't trust her. Her eyes only lit on him and he wondered if he failed, would they finally forgive her for saving him that night of dark moons so long ago. Would she be better if he just let the dead reclaim his father's ka for their own?

"Begin the climb," the elder called, silencing the songs. They would have the day to climb to the bottom, capture the sea in a cliff flower gourde, then climb back up, chose a cave to make prayer in and dump the water from the sea as an offering to the dead. If they did that and climbed back, they'd be full members of the village.

Acceptance seemed a great gift to Shine, though he imagined even if he did things their way, within the tradition, even full adulthood wouldn't mean acceptance for him. Too many children went to the dead on moonless nights for that to be.

The other two, scrambled over the side of the cliff and made their way down, pace careful but quick, showing how they'd trained long for this.

Shine waited until the villagers crowded along the curve of the cliff, watching the others, then he put his fingers to his lips and whistled a shrill note. The others, murmuring among themselves about Cleon and Jorcer's speed or agility, stopped for a moment and looked up. Shine's gaze pointed toward his hut where the others looked to see what he watched. From behind it, a creature lumbered, gait oddly rolling under the points of its bone white legs. Bone white because it was made of bone. Bone and sinews stretched with dried out muscle knotting it together. Spindle legs trotted forward carrying a curved back and shortened forearms the ended in sharp bone hooks. Atop the creature's long, curving neck, a skull with a lengthy snout, side set eyes, high earholes, and white canine teeth.

It lumbered over to him and rubbed its bone snout against his knotted climbing gear. Shine smiled and ran his hand across the creature's skull between the eyeholes.

"I made you," he said, then pulled himself up onto

its back, into the spread-out seat made by a gap in its ridged vertebra. "Let's go."

The villagers watched, stunned in silence, as Shine and his beast hobbled over the edge of the cliff. Though the thing wasn't graceful on the even ground of the clifftop village, once they turned and clambered backward over the cliff's edge, the thing's pointed back feet and shortened fore-hooks perfectly scaled the cliff, nimbly hopping and grabbing holds and ledges without err. Soon, Shine passed the other two twelves, slowly making their way down the cliff face with the efforts of their own fingers and muscles and bones.

Cleon's cruel face turned to him, his mouth an o of shock and eyes angry, but such things he put aside as Shine passed him with a gentle hop and scrabble that carried him twenty feet in a minute.

The climb, something that should have taken all day, took minutes and soon he stood at the foot of the cliff where the green sea met the rock. With his gourd he scooped up the water, amazed at how warm it was. How soft on his skin. He thought, I'll make something that will let us swim the sea someday.

And his ka sang with the thought.

He mounted his creature and again they climbed, as easy as the down trip they went back up. Hooked beastie snorted and clucked with a pleasure only a maker might understand, joy in its every step and breath of new life. Parts working together though in life they'd been in five different beasts.

Soon they passed the other two, still climbing down.

Jorcer body shook with the trembles of her efforts and she spared just one glance at him, the first he'd ever gotten. In her eyes, he read respect, not fear and thought perhaps, if she survived, they might someday call each other friend.

Still he climbed, his beast picking through the banks of cliff flowers, never disturbing a root or fruit.

Shine hoped the villages could see his creation's beauty and not just its strangeness.

Then he stopped at the mouth of cave of the dead, sliding from the bone back of his beast. The thing refused to be left behind, walking with him into the dark mouth of the cave. It pressed its tall side against his shoulder, lending strength to its creator. Shine's pride at his making filled him with courage. He was a child of the dark moons, given new life as this creature of his was. They would probe the dark together.

Ahead of them, a light flickered.

Ahead of them, the truth.

He'd not just dump his water and run. He'd know the caves for himself.

***

By the time he was done exploring with his creature, the other twelves had caught up, poured their water, and begun the ascent back to the village. Shine mounted the beast and saw them up above him, laboring up though the sheerest part of the climb. Once the beast began climbing, they passed the two within a few easy minutes and up over the lip of the cliff.

Larmer ran for him, throwing her arms around him.

"I thought you'd left me for the dead," she whispered into his ear. "You were in there so long."

The villagers gathered around them, hanging back from the odd creature. The chants they usually gave the first twelve over the side dried up in their mouths like dust as they watched him.

Always watching.

He turned, cleared his throat, hoping he'd create words as well as creatures.

"I have gifts for you," he said, laying his hand on the beastie. "This creature is willing to help us farm. He and the others I can make will keep us safe from falls. There will be no more lost like my da."

Still watching, though hands folded over hearts as memories of those lost to the sea welled up in him.

"I am a creator, not a farmer. If you will have me, I will create for you. Make our lives better."

Suspicion. The dead told him that they'd not believe, even with the creature before them, ready to work.

"This is sacrilege," Cleon's father said, clutching his exhausted son to him. The boy had just climbed over and mumbled about Shine cheating him out of glory.

The others nodded and pressed in, fear overriding sense as it often did.

"Don't you wish to know what the dead taught me in the cave?" He bellowed over their raised voices and complaints.

"I want to know," Larmer said, voice tossed above the others, a seabird on a storm.

The grumbling quieted some, but not enough. Not enough to be heard.

"I want to hear him," Jorcer said, pulling herself up over the edge. She stood as strong as she had when she started, muscles shining with the sheen of exertion. She'd done the climb without show and without pain. She'd made it and she deserved a hearing. "I saw him enter. I went into the cave he chose and left before he came out. I know he went in deep to the dead. I want to know what they taught."

The village respected Jorcer's hard work and her lack of show. When she spoke, they believed her words even though until that day she'd been but a child. With the force of the climb behind her, all quieted.

They would listen.

Shine took a deep breath, knowing that he couldn't reveal all. The farm folk needed some truth. But all truths had to be saved for the seekers. There was one thing the dead wanted them to know.

"The nights of the dark moon, when you put the babies out for the dead, they take them only because they know you will not have them back. Because you think you understand. Because you never bother to ask them."

As he spoke, he turned toward the cliff.

Something moved there, at the edge.

"The world of the dead isn't all dead."

White hands with snaggled, desiccated skin reached over the side, grasping at clumps of saw grass to pull up.

"Beneath us they live in the caves, a beautiful city of honeycombed caves and they care for the children you've abandoned."

The dead men and women from the cave city pulled themselves over the side, clinging on their backs were live children of all ages. Some grown live people climbed over and stood, shoulder to shoulder to the many dead. A crowd of them gathered behind Shine and the creature, staring over the distance to the live villagers. The dead's creaky voices whispered to the live in their ranks. The live children and grown men clutched the hands of the dead closest to them, hugged them. Whispered things. Then the live ones, crossed the distance.

"The dead wish to return your children to you. They wish them to live in the light."

Several of the villagers sobbed as the live children found them, embraced them and called them their Da and Ma.

Shine didn't know if his gifts would be accepted or if later the villages would revert to their old ways.

What he did know was that the dead accepted him even if the village didn't and that his creations would be useful. He rubbed his hands on his creature who nuzzled him with his jagged muzzle.

"You deserve a name, my friend," he told him. "I will call you Miracle."

Warning
Sarah Cannavo

Hold your breath passing cemeteries
for fear of offending the dead;
to breathe is to brag, flaunting
it to those who can't, a
reminder they won't
take kindly to
(or so the
ghosts told
    me).

Cry of the Banshee
Denise Noe

What is the cry of the banshee?
What could that shriek possibly be?
But Jepthah's burnt offering,
A child who could never sing.
The child he was sworn to kill
A sacrificed child who still
Yearns for a universe she can never see
Her spirit still mourning her virginity.

"Funeral of Mankind" by Sonali Roy

Article

Great and Terrible: An Examination of Jonathan Edwards', "Sinners in the Hands of an Angry God" Through the Lens of Cosmic Horror.

Anthony Perconti

About twenty-five years ago, as an undergraduate, I had the privilege of taking a requisite course entitled Survey of American Literature, Section One. In this class, we read and examined a variety of early American fiction and nonfiction alike. There were two pieces in particular, that had a quite an impact on me. One was Nathaniel Hawthorne's "The Minister's Black Veil"; a tale of Mr. Hooper, the Reverend of a small Puritan New England town, ever ensconced in a black veil that hides his visage. All throughout his life, Reverend Hooper views the temporal world through the lens of this black veil. As striking and fatalistic as this story and its accompanying imagery was, it paled in comparison to the sermon by Jonathan Edwards, entitled "Sinners in the Hands of an Angry God". The Edwards sermon was like nothing I'd ever encountered before; it did not compute with my version of Christianity. At roughly the same time, I received my first exposure to the works of Howard Phillips Lovecraft as well. At my local Barnes and Noble, I picked up the superlative, *The Annotated H.P. Lovecraft* (edited by ST Joshi). After digesting both the Edwards sermon and Joshi's *The Annotated H.P. Lovecraft*, I came to the realization that Edward's version of Christianity and God disturbed me a sight more than the entities that premiered in the pages of Weird Tales. This on its face seems preposterous. How can a religion that I am part of, be more terrifying that eldritch space gods? It is my contention that it is a matter of intent.

The 1741, Great Awakening sermon, "Sinners in the Hands of an Angry God", works profoundly well as a cautionary tract. The vast majority of the sermon is comprised of ten 'considerations' that state in no uncertain terms what fate will befall all sinners and unbelievers. Consideration number ten for example, succinctly sums up the gist of Edwards' sermon. "God has laid himself under no obligation, by any promise to keep any natural man out of hell one moment. God certainly has made no promises either of eternal life, or of any deliverance or preservation from eternal death, but what are contained in the covenant of grace, the promises that are given in Christ, in whom all the promises are yea and amen." (1.) The remaining nine considerations are certainly of a piece with the aforementioned tenth. The choice is always binary and the outcome (paradoxically, from a human standpoint) is already known. The most striking aspect of the Edwards sermon lies in its ability to instill a sense of holy terror within its listeners (and readers). This version of God is more akin to its ancient Mesopotamian progenitors; all powerful, all knowing and quite vengeful. The options are very clear according to Edwards. Repent your sins, accept Jesus into your life as the savior, or else be banished to eternal damnation. In Edwards' worldview, there is absolutely no room for theological nuance or discourse; it is obey or die.

The literary philosophy of Cosmicism was conceived by the American pulp writer, H.P. Lovecraft. This philosophy's main conceit states that humanity is of little consequence when compared to the greater universe. The entirety of human history and civilization is merely a blip in the vastness of cosmological space and time. C.R. Wiley states; "Summed up briefly, Cosmicism is based on the idea that humanism is an illusion. Human consciousness, human civilization, humane values, and all the rest, add up to a bubble that surrounds us and keeps us from seeing that the cosmos is wholly indifferent to us. (Interesting word choice there by Lovecraft.) It's not that it is necessarily hostile, although it might seem that way. It's just that in the vast sweep of time and space, human beings are nothing. We have our time on this speck of a planet, but there were eons before we arrived, and there will be eons after we're gone. The abyss surrounds us." (2.) This is not an optimistic viewpoint by any stretch of the imagination.

The sub-genre of cosmic horror is directly derived from this literary philosophy. In cosmic horror, the true terror stems from the fact that human beings are an incidental species at best. Humanity is so infinitesimal (and so short lived) that when it encounters the larger forces of the cosmos, they reel in terror at the sense of immensity and scale. The cosmological beings that populate Lovecraft's fiction are not necessarily taking direct action against our species. They are not precisely malign towards us, because frankly, we do not register to them. We are so small in comparison, that we cannot pose anything resembling a threat to them. We as individuals don't declare all-out war against our skin's microbiome, do we? The same can be said of these cosmological forces. If nothing else, it is a backhanded reassurance that the cosmos is indifferent to us; in that, it is not *openly hostile* towards our species. Lovecraft's bookish protagonists always descend into madness when they encounter forces from The Outside; it is important to note however, that these entities are not in an antagonistic relationship with us, per se. It is the individual's limited and finite set of sensory tools that fail them.

Human beings are not capable of processing beyond our scale. This madness is derived from a massive dose of existential anomie. "Human attempts to transform the alien entities into gods are clearly regarded by Lovecraft as vain acts of anthropomorphism, perhaps noble but ultimately absurd efforts to impose meaning and sense on to the "real externality" of a cosmos in which human concerns, perspectives and concepts have only a local reference." (3.)

Growing up in northern New Jersey, as the son of Italian immigrants, the symbols and rituals of our religion were always around us, within reach. Christmas Eve and Christmas Day dinners are still long, drawn out affairs that test the diner's eating endurance (these take place after mass, of course). We would have several representations of Jesus, the Crucifix and The Madonna strategically placed throughout our home, to make the most impact on the family members. Da Vinci's The Last Supper hung over our kitchen table, wreathed in a shell fringed frame (straight from the island of Sicily). My mother in those days certainly had an eye for the dramatic, to be sure. The most impressive icon we had was a beautifully rendered portrait of the (lily white) Son of Man, at his most mercifully majestic, arms open wide, giving off an aura of divinity, which gave the optical illusion, that his sky-blue eyes followed you wherever in the room you went. Unsettling, to be sure, but I never felt that stare to be malign; after all (according to Father Dante), Jesus loves us all. My mother, even to this day, is a staunch, practicing, Roman Catholic, who still *tisks* at me for not taking her grandsons to mass on Sundays (she has given up on me, but she still keeps me in her nightly prayers). Maternal guilt aside, being reared in the Catholic tradition in the post Second

Vatican Council era, I never once felt that the figure of Jesus, or his Old Testament sire, had any cruel designs on my soul. The mere fact of Vatican Two's existence, planed down the more (jagged) draconian aspects of Christian (or to be more precise, Catholic) dogma.

Jonathan Edwards' iteration of God is entirely outside of my religious experience. If you can imagine an entity that is responsible for the creation of the totality of the universe and make that said being insanely draconian and paranoid, that in a nutshell, encapsulates the God from "Sinners". I cannot fathom a deity that is so disdainful of its creations, so jealous, with such a brittle ego, that in a backwater galaxy (amidst the cosmological expanse of the universe), it keeps tabs on the individual doings of what amount to be dust mites. And by this logic, this God is doing the exact same thing simultaneously across the myriad planets that sustain life. At the very least, the creatures found in Lovecraft are basically indifferent to our race. Edwards' God is always watching and waiting. At a moment's displeasure, sinners are shunted off, for all eternity to Hell. What makes this scenario more disturbing, is the fact that we as finite creatures cannot possibly conceive, let alone comprehend, the plans of a being that is infinite; Its motivations and whims are opaque from our standpoint. What may seem a perfectly routine action to us, could be to the eyes of God, a damnable offense. Even with the roadmap presented to the listener on how not to offend God and end up eternally damned, it is at best, drastically faded and unclear. Edwards' fundamentalist brand of Christianity is to my eyes, a zero-sum game; there is no room for nuance or examination in this authoritarian branch of the tree. I would like to think that an omnipotent being, would come to appreciate (or at least, be amused by) such traits as intelligent discourse, adaptability of thinking, subtlety and existential questioning, in its creation. Much like a proud parent would be of a child who posited and expressed a sophisticated thought.

The God portrayed in "Sinners" has less in common with the Lovecraftian pantheon than it does with the creation of British fantasist, Michael Moorcock's, Lords of Chaos. These cosmic beings treat worlds as their personal playthings. Humanity (and other sentient beings) is merely another pawn in their never-ending, inscrutable cosmological games. One Lord in particular, Arioch (the patron of the doomed albino emperor, Elric), strikes me as kith and kin to Edwards' deity. "And then the full injustice of his fate struck him. Arioch bore no malice towards the Vadhagh. He cared for them no more nor less than he cared for the Mabden parasites feeding off his body. He was merely wiping his palate clean of old colors as a painter will before he begins a fresh canvas. All the agony and the misery he and his had suffered was on behalf of the whim of a careless God who only occasionally turned his attention to the world that he had been given to rule." (4.) With a slight addendum; it seems as though Edwards' version of God bears a *greater degree* of malice towards unrepentant sinners. This God's attention is constantly on its creation; ever poised to cast down unbelievers whenever the fancy strikes.

I was presented at a formative age with a variety of viewpoints on religion and our place in the cosmos. I consider this a privilege, in that, it shaped the way I look at the world and my place within it. The empirical, logical part of my mind finds much merit in Lovecraft's ideology. It makes sense to me on a rational level, given what science has shown us of the universe. And yet, another part of me finds comfort in the traditions associated with Southern European Roman Catholicism. I understand that on a fundamental level, these two viewpoints do not jibe, that they are mutually exclusive. These diametrically opposing modes of thought both serve a purpose in my life; they provide me with logical and emotional sustenance. The same cannot be said of Edwards' vision of Christianity. It espouses Lovecraft's sense of humankind's insignificance, coupled with the more authoritarian aspects of Christian teachings. As an adult, I have no problem living with and synthesizing opposing philosophies, but this ideology is a bridge too far for my taste. It is far too rigid and stifling; both from an emotional as well as a logical perspective.

Notes
1. Edwards, Johnathan, "Sinners in the Hands of an Angry God" (Osnova Publications, 1835) 17%.
2. Wiley, C.R., "Lovecraft's Cosmicism: What it Is, How It Works, and Why It Fails", patheos.com, August, 24, 2017, https://www.patheos.com/blogs/gloryseed/2017/08/1ovecrafts-cosmicism-works-fails/.
3. Fisher, Mark, *The Weird and the Eerie* (London: Repeater Books, 2016) p. 18.
4. Moorcock, Michael, *The Swords Trilogy* (New York: Berkley Medallion Books, 1971) p. 134.

Bibliography
Edwards, Johnathan. "Sinners in the Hands of an Angry God". Osnova Publications. 1835
Fisher, Mark. *The Weird and the Eerie.* London: Repeater Books. 2016
Moorcock, Michael. *The Swords Trilogy.* New York: Berkley Medallion Books. 1971
Wiley, C.R. "Lovecraft's Cosmicism: What it Is, How It Works, and Why It Fails". patheos.com. 2017

Article

Plunging into the Mystery of Automatic or Mediumistic Art & Artists...
Sonali Roy

Spirits appeared and inspired people earlier. So, there were and still are great mediums and clairvoyants. Mediums are also said to have plunged into artistic endeavors guided by spirits, apparitions, deities, and legendary characters, whose presence may be weird to other people. In most of the cases, such artists didn't have enough knowledge of the particular culture & thoughts they were inspired of. They drew quite spontaneously as if they didn't even feel the need for mindfulness about what they painted. You may call their creation as something originating from the richness of their inner self. And most interestingly, many of them didn't have professional or formal training as an artist- they initiated artistic projects that sometimes they drew inspiration from spirits and sometimes by genetic influence and portrayed some unfamiliar faces, forms, shapes, and characters independent of their consciousness. Skeptics and some commoners may doubt about all these that people with a very limited number are gifted with such divine talent. But, such divine people, through their mediumistic power, were able to talk about life after death, the interconnectedness to the celestial, and the necessity to lead a life that could please the Almighty.

Alma Rumball (1902-1980), hailing from Canada, a mediumistic artist living in rural Huntsville, Ontario, created lots of fascinating drawings as motivated by the creative forces/and the Christ. As Alma shares in the documentary film 'The Alma Drawings', she was in touch with the Christ energy- she says, "That's Christ. I've seen his face many times; he isn't wearing his whiskers though you know." Accordingly, Alma's physical hands recorded only what the spiritual forces/the holy Christ energy/and the Holy Ghost instructed her to do- she translated their messages and images. That's why she never claimed the authorship of her drawings. She said, "I can't accept credit for them; you see, I don't do them." Alma just drew inspiration from her visions as she wanted to keep creating. She said, "I just had to keep going, that's all. I hardly had time to finish one picture and my Hand started another one." Alma became a mediumistic artist at the age of 50. Though with limited training, Alma produced wonderful pencil sketches, wax & crayon images, weird hieroglyphics sometimes outlined with black ink and sometimes with the text involvement. For instance, think of 'Alma Came To Earth as Joan of Arc' and 'Many Ghosts Are Alive But Are Controlled by God'. Besides, she wrote about over two hundred pages on the lost civilization of Atlantis, where she included some abstract sketches above each page. She also produced with the colorful metallic ink that gave the bright fluorescent effect alongside the golden & silver touch-up to her drawings. Though she had no previous knowledge about eastern culture and beliefs, Alma included references to these as she could not realize the source of her works. Her works were motivated by Tibetan symbols and deities, images of Atlantis, and Joan of Arc. Alma also owes much to her spiritual guide Aba Pasha, a black, turbaned man, for her otherwordly creation. On the whole, Alma incorporated the psychic automatism. As Michael Greenwood, who curated for Toronto's York University Art Gallery and organized Alma's first major 'one woman show' in 1978, wrote, "History records many instances of the phenomenon of automatism in the production of art works, though seldom found in so pure a form as in Alma Rumball's drawings." Moreover, Alma's drawings and texts convey a message to this world that we should change ourselves, else, we could be destined to the similar as of the lost civilization of Atlantis.

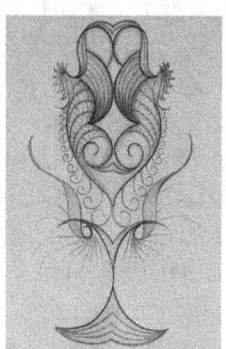

Anna Hackel or **Haskel** hailing from a humble Bohemian farming background was born in August 1864. Anna's life was a 'varitable channel-house littered with deadbodies' that made her lonely at a very earlier stage of life. Say of the deaths of her parents, her husband, or her children- all contributed to her hardship that she realized her artistic passion guided by the higher power at her fifties and created colorful floral sketches that would certainly make you curious about her style and inspiration. A larger portion of her works came out in the 1930s. Anna created thousands of works and attended many exhibitions. She said, "I do not need to concentrate on my work, but can talk and otherwise occupy myself at the same time." She never felt the need for mindfulness for her creation. She created colorful spirals, geometric shapes, and arabesques as guided by highly spiritual power and art.

Mediumistic artist **Wilhelmine Assmann** from Germany lived in between 1867-1943. Widely exhibited in France, Germany, Holland, and the UK, Assmann led a life of hardships and works that she was the daughter of a poor miner and also married a poor man. Her bewildering bold trance creations of minute details include floral patterns and geometrical forms that often perplexed great scientists and doctors of Germany. Most interestingly, Assmann never spent her hours in formal training of art though spent nearly 50 hours on a single painting.

The great psychic artist, author, and the first female dentist in Bay City, **Marian Spore Bush**, lived in between 1878-1946 and attended the University of Michigan School of Dentistry as Flora Mae Spore. A pioneer in the periodontal dentistry, Spore Bush, was widely known in Bay City for her excellent work that she devised inlays, crowns, bridgework, and dental plates in her own laboratory. She was also known for her charity that she gave out $40,000 worth of meal vouchers and clothing yearly throughout the Great Depression (1929-1939) that stirred the world on economical front.

Her psychic and naive paintings often feature birds and surrealism. Marian connected to the other worldly through the Ouija board that helped her much in her creative endeavors. With the Ouija, she felt as if like connecting to her mother's spirit. Not only that, it seemed to her the dead artists or 'they' inspired her for her surreal and symbolical painting and that she tried oil painting. Most importantly, Marian called the dead artists as 'they' for the rest of her life. She also penned a memoir titled as 'They' published posthumously in 1947. Her notable works are Huts and Palm Trees, Guam Seascape, Temple of the Goddess of Flowers, Temple of Priests of the Poisonous Faith of the East, The Temple of Snakes, The Temple of the Sun Worshippers, The Temple of Far Away India, Temple by the Sea, The Temple of the Sea God Neptune, Asian Inspired House, Swans, Three Fish, Waterfowl, Roses, and many.

Another mediumistic artist **Gertrud Emde** living in between 1929-2019 in Ottobrunn near Munich with her husband Dr. Gunter Emde, a physicist, and their two children, was passionate about spiritualism, parapsychology, and transcendent sciences. Gertrud was gifted with writing and drawing mediumistically. Her talent began flourishing in 1979, when her creative hands, instead of writing, gave rise to her surprise to automatic productions of drawings full of greater faith and knowledge with wax crayons and watercolors. As time passed by, Gertrud created much more with her passionate, observant, mediumistic eyes full of precognition of dreams and prayers to God that she also utilized while teaching spiritual lessons and working as a healer. She had wonderful and fascinating geometrical and floral creation of automatic paintings making people convince of a higher world as inspired by the spiritual entities including a male and a female respectively.

credit: Christian Berst

Mediumistic and visionary artist **Madge Gill** (1882-1961) guided by a spirit called Myrninerest was famous for her sketching of faces of nameless women floating ethereally. For her art, Gill often used silk, rugs, and even her own clothes, on which, she created visionary drawings and knittings. She also created on postcards and pieces of cupboards. Without any prior knowledge of art, Madge gave rise to a spontaneous and effortless flow of creation full of symbols and words along with biblical and astrological references. In the latest biography 'The Life of Madge Gill', Roger Cardinal, a surreal enthusiast coining the term 'Outsider Art' in 1972, wrote, "Gill's frenetic improvizations have an almost hallucinatory quality, each surface being filled with checkerboard patterns that suggest giddy, quasi-architectural spaces. Afloat upon these swirling proliferations are the pale faces of discarnate and nameless women, sketched perfunctorily, albeit with an apparent concern for beauty, and with startled expressions."

Visionary artist **Marguerite Burnat-Provins**, the descendant to an intellectual family, coming of a Belgian father and a Dutch mother on June 26, 1872 in Arras, France, studied art and at the age of twenty four, married a Swiss architect Adolphe Burnat-Provins. Marguerite continued her education and established herself as a reputed author and painter. On one occasion, she saw and drew 48 visions in a single sitting. As per the observation of the psychical investigator Dr. Eugene Osty, "One might say they are elements of social life; parts played by individuals in the surroundings of city life; morphological or moral forms, the diverse forms of destiny, all the types of human activity, and figurative of beliefs, superstitions, defects, and qualities, and many personifications of Nature – the seasons, the wind and so forth. Mme. Burnat-Provins gives the name Ma Ville to the people of her visions in human beings, animals, allegories, things, and events happening in a dream-town, a dream with marvellously co-ordinated episodes."

Dr. Osty recorded, "What does Mme. Burnat-Provins think, and how does she explain her visions? This very intelligent artist refrains from an opinion unless forced. If pressed she says: "In style, workmanship, and aspect this production has no relation with my other work as a painter. I could not, were it for a fortune, draw any of these heads to order. Usually these figures are ugly, even hideous; those that are beautiful or even endurable, are few, and all that they represent is opposed to the turn of my mind which has always sought for beauty and harmony. My work as a writer shows this. The idea of subconscious creation suggests itself, because the part that this has played in my life is well known. In this matter, I reject that idea because I feel the contrary. I neither desire, nor feel moved to call or create these personages. Most of them are antipathetic or odious to me. I submit to them, I feel them come like a burden, but cannot refuse to draw them."

Further Readings:

http://www.almamatters.ca/
https://musee.mahhsa.fr/artiste/anna-hackel-haskel/
https://mariansporebush.com/
https://madgegill.com/
https://www.artbrut.ch/en_GB/author/burnat-provins-marguerite
https://mediumisticart.com/artists-mediumistic-psychic-visionary-spiritual/marguerite-burnat-provins/
https://www.collegeofpsychicstudies.co.uk/on-demand/spirit-inspired-art/automatic-drawings-of-alma-rumball/

–

ARTICLE

Joyce Carol Oates's Second Exploration of Grotesquerie: *The Collector of Hearts*
Denise Noe

This essay examines how Joyce Carol Oates explores the "grotesque" in *The Collector of Hearts: New Tales of the Grotesque.* In her previous *Haunted: Tales of the Grotesque,* Oates wrote in an afterword,

> "I take it as the most profound mystery of our human experience that, though we each exist subjectively, and know the world only through the prism of self, this 'subjectivity' is inaccessible, thus unreal, and mysterious to others. . . . all *others* are, in the deepest sense, *strangers.*"

She suggests this mystery feeds the "grotesque."

Collector's first story is "The Sky Blue Ball." The unnamed narrator is an adult recounting an incident that occurred when she was fourteen. She walked beside a brick wall when a ball "so brightly blue" she initially mistook it for a bird sailed by. She fetched it. The ball "looked new, smelled new, spongy and resilient in my hand like a rubber ball I'd played with years before as a little girl." She tossed it over the wall; it was thrown back. Surmising the person returning the ball is another kid, probably a girl younger than herself, she repeatedly called but heard nothing back.

The ball was thrown at an "unexpected angle," leading her to rush into the road, hearing "the ugly shriek of brakes and a deafening angry horn" before falling and badly scraping her knees. Again she threw the ball but it was not thrown back. Disheartened by her emotional investment in this game, she thought,

> "It seemed silly and contemptible to me, and sad: there I stood . . . a long-limbed weed of a girl . . . panting and bleeding from the knees, the palms of my hands, too, chafed and scraped and dirty; there I stood alone in front of a moldering brick wall waiting for — what?"

She felt driven to find playmate and/or ball. She put an oil drum against the wall, climbed on it, jumped over the wall. Landing, she felt as "if I'd been struck a sledgehammer blow to the soles of my feet." She realized "there could be no little girl here, the factory yard was surely deserted." Even as she finds the yard empty, she realizes there is a "normal" explanation: "The child had drifted away, I supposed; she'd lost interest in our game." But there seems no normal explanation for the way she finds the ball transformed: "no longer sky blue but faded and cracked; its dun-colored rubber showed through the venous-cracked surface, like my own ball, years ago."

"The Sky Blue Ball" is superficially banal and I believe deliberately so. Indeed, it is my belief that Oates began this *New Tales of the Grotesque* in part to challenge reader assumptions about what constitutes literary grotesquerie. "The Sky Blue Ball" demands that we search for what is grotesque in it. It reward that search by leading the reader to the truth that the story *is* grotesque. In minutes the ball changed from brightly colored to dull. The ball is tossed back by someone who might not even exist.

Perhaps a younger version of herself visited the narrator. Perhaps the narrator retrieved the ball to retrieve her earlier childhood. Searching for the grotesque lurking within "The Sky Blue Ball" leads us to recognize how horror can lie beneath the everyday.

Haunted Childhoods, Parental Deaths

"Death Mother" and "Schroeder's Stepfather" feature adults haunted by childhood abuse. The first focuses on coed Jeannette Harth whose mother suffered a mental breakdown that triggered violence. Mom killed Jeannette's sister Mary, then took Jeannette on a ride meant to end with murder-suicide. But both survived.

Jeannette is surprised to find Mom released from the psychiatric hospital where she had been held for years. A confluence of contradictory emotions overcome Jeannette upon seeing the woman who gave her life, then attempted to take it, the woman who killed her sister. They try to act "normal" as they chat, that very normalcy rendered grotesque by their history.

The final grotesquerie occurs on the last page: Jeannette will not be able to repair the mother-daughter relationship. Mom dies when her car plunges off a bridge. Suicide? Accident? There is no way to know. But the echo adds another layer of the grotesque to the history that haunts Jeannette.

In "Schroeder's Stepfather," John is haunted by memories of abuse by step-father Jack. One morning, the men accompany each other to examine hurricane damage inflicted on Jack's property. During the drive, John reminds Jack of the harsh teasing and punishments John suffered as a child at the hands of his step-dad; he reminds Jack that he mistreated John's dog so badly the creature died. Jack claims no memory of these events.

John's childhood memories are ambiguous. He recalls Jack insisting the lad accompany him to the cellar where Jack insisted John pull down his pants for a spanking. Was it just a spanking? Whether or not there was also sexual abuse is open. We also wonder if the insistence that it be on the bare bottom indicated a sexual motivation.

When the men see the damaged property "the sight of his badly battered shingle board cottage and dock so upset the elder Schroeder that he died on the debris-strewn bench: collapsed, fell dead within minutes."

A doctor diagnoses death by cardiac failure. But Oates suggests uncertainty, stating Jack fell down,

> "John's sudden foot on the nape of [Jack's] beefy neck urging his face into the sand with the hope of smothering him (for is not smothering of all strategies of homicide the most difficult to detect? Diagnosed usually as 'cardiac failure'?) was unnecessary: except as a final gesture."

In any intimate relationship, polarized emotions of love and hate, fear and dependence, caring and resentment co-exist. In relationships like those between Jeannette and her mother, Jack and his step-father, the negative emotions have been grotesquely exaggerated.

There is a difference in the stories. "Death Mother's" ending suggests Jeannette will be haunted by the grotesquerie of her mother's mental illness and violence but we also know Jeannette is a survivor who will persevere. She will not be *as* haunted by her mother's death as John is apt to be haunted by Jack's since Jeannette neither contributed to her Mom's death nor fantasized that she did. John, haunted by childhood torments, is apt to spend the rest of his life even more haunted by his possible role in Jack's death.

Oates has stated,

"I am especially interested in how people, especially women and children, cope with the aftermath of violence."

"Death Mother" and "Schroeder's Stepfather" exemplify this special interest as they depict children who grew into adults who had to find ways to "cope with the aftermath of violence." The stories also deal with the inevitably conflicting feelings that surround violence between people who know each, especially people who are intimates and linked by blood or marriage. Jeannette and her sister Mary were given life by the very person who took Mary's life and tried to take Jeannette's life. The fuzziness of memory and of perception are illustrated by John's story, by his recalling discipline that may or may not have been abusive and may or may not have possessed a sexual motivation.

Grotesque Puppets

Few things possess the inherent grotesquerie of puppets. Many horror stories feature puppets coming to life or taking over the lives of the humans who speak through them. This legacy informs Oates's "The Hand-puppet."

Oates begins: "*How strangeness enters our lives.*" The lives described appear models of normality. Lorraine Lake is a married suburban mom living, her husband away on business. Daughter Tippi is a shy 11-year-old. Lorraine is startled to hear "H'LO MISSUS! G'MORNING' MISSUS!" A puppet is thrust before her from a closet door. The puppet has a "leering red-satin mouth" with a "body made of stiff felt that was mainly shoulders and arms; the head was bald and domed, like an embryo's." Mom remonstrates with the girl about scaring "your poor mother." In "a low guttural drawl," Tippi continues, "MISSUS I BEEN HERE BEFORE YA! AN' I GONNA BE HERE WHENYA GONE!"

Lorraine is impressed by Tippi's crafting and baffled by how effectively the child changed her voice. Tippi dismisses the puppet as "some silly thing I made" and says she will not take it to school.

After Tippi goes to school, the child's ventriloquism haunts Lorraine, the words playing repeatedly in her head: "MISSUS I BEEN HERE BEFORE YA! AN' I GONNA BE HERE WHENYA GONE!" The sentence, "*How strangeness enters our lives,*" recurs in Lorraine's mind. In the middle of the day, Lorraine drives by Tippi's school. Spotting Tippi on the playground, Lorraine is startled that Tippi *has* brought the puppet to school. Lorraine is even more disconcerted to see Tippi "advancing aggressively" toward younger children and "wielding the puppet like a weapon." Tippi appears to use the puppet to release aggressions against younger children, playing on the "grotesque" truth that people often take their frustrations out on those weaker.

Lorraine bounces between "that child is mad" and "it's harmless, just a game."

Concern about the puppet is paralleled by Lorraine's concern about her own medical problems. She makes a doctor's appointment where she learns that she has a tumor in her womb and this necessitates a hysterectomy. This introduces the possibility that Lorraine's anxiety about her medical issues is being displaced onto Tippi's "silly" puppetry.

At home, Lorraine ruminates whether to confront Tippi for lying about taking the puppet to school. Lorraine decides she does not want the confrontation. Lorraine goes to the attic, "a place of sanctuary, solitude. The sky was closer here." The story ends with Lorraine staring through the window at "impacted clouds," imagining "climbing into the sky of boulders."

Once again, Oates plays with our expectations and deliberately frustrates them. Oates does not have the puppet "possess" the child or come alive. Rather, Oates leaves the nature of the "strangeness" tantalizingly open. The "strangeness" that has entered Lorraine Lake's life could be the knowledge of her ordinary child's unusual talents or her child's unexpected and even frightening aggressiveness. The "strangeness" could only be her fears about her health that she has displaced onto a puppet. The story raises multiple questions and "grotesquely" refuses to answer them.

Slivers of Darkness Obscure Haunting Memories

One story has no word title. A black rectangle is put in as the title so I will call it "Black Rectangle." It is narrated by a woman recalling a childhood episode of visiting rich relatives, Uncle Rebhorn, Aunt Elinor, cousins Audrey and Darren. She recalls "at the center of what happened on that Sunday many years ago is . . . . this black rectangle . . . and at the center of my girlhood."

The home's attractive exterior curiously contrasted with its interior: "It was the most beautiful house I was ever to enter. Three stories high, broad and gleaming pale-pink." She continues, "As we approached the big front door which was made of carved wood, with a beautiful gleaming brass American eagle, its dimensions seemed to shrink; the closer we got, the smaller the door got." Then: "to enter Uncle Rebhorn's sandstone mansion . . . we had to crouch. And push and squeeze our shoulders through the doorway."

The entrance constitutes "a kind of tunnel" in which everyone must walk "on our haunches in a squatting position."

The group eats lunch in a "room crowded with cartons and barrels," sitting "on packing cases." The meal is "tough, bright pink meat curling at the edges and leaking blood, and puddles of corn pudding . . . in a runny pale sauce like pus."

Dessert is singularly grotesque. At first, the girl thinks it "apple jelly" but finds her "spoon wasn't sharp enough to cut into the jelly." Laughingly, Uncle Rebhorn asks, "You don't think your dessert is a *jellyfish*, do you?"

She realizes "that was exactly what it was: a jellyfish. Each of us had one, in our bowls. Warm and pulsing with life and fear radiating from it like raw nerves."

The group goes sailing. Young Darren falls into the water, barely missing being drowned.

Throughout the story the narrator tells us that this was a pivotal day in her life . . . but she does not know what exactly made it pivotal. Parts of her memory — perhaps the most significant parts — are lost. But there are clues to the drastic nature of those forgotten events. Uncle Rebhorn teases her as a "naughty girl." Later: "*I am not a naughty girl* I wanted to protest and now too *I am not to blame.*" And later: "*I am not to blame, I am not deserving of hurt neither then nor now* but do I believe this, even if I can succeed in making you believe it?" And also later: *"if there is a God in heaven please forgive me."* We are told Uncle Rebhorn "was on the other side of the door" and both the narrator and Audrey heard "his harsh labored breathing" before he said, "D-you naughty little girls need any help getting your panties down? or your bathing suits on?" Then there is the scene of the almost drowning of cousin Darren from the boat. What else happened? "Slivers of blackness" obscure memory.

Oates writes powerfully of how perceptions and memories become seriously distorted. A memory that is agonizingly painful may be repressed, lost, obscured as part of the mind tries to protect itself from horror. Yet the person who cannot remember is not left free, only confused as is the narrator of "Black Rectangle," saddled with a terrible guilt, forever confused about its true source.

Power Abused Grotesquerie

The story that gives the collection its name, "The Collector of Hearts," begins: "Funny! You never met me, don't know my name but you're holding me in your hand. Turning me in your fingers, peering at what remains of me saying *This is – ivory? Carved? It's so beautiful.*" The narrator of this paragraph is apparently an elephant's ghost.

Oates switches to a young African-American woman narrator who has had brushes with the law. That morning, she stood before a judge for shoplifting, bad checks, and assault. She got "in a scuffle with the security guard" at a store "where he'd insulted me with a racial epithet so I went a little wild and bit the fucker in the hand." Believing the judge sympathetic, she pleads guilty. "Eight months, suspended sentence," he ruled. She hoped "there was this special understanding between us *because I was special*" even as she realizes this is something "we all know or wish to believe in our hearts."

The judge who showed leniency invites her to his home. He shows her his collection of heart shaped craft objects. The reader recalls the first paragraph when she describes "an exquisitely carved ivory heart." She touches a "handle of wood" possessing a heart "fine-carved to resemble an actual heart with veins." The grotesquerie startles when she elaborates, "I had a weird sensation almost like . . . inside the carved wood heart it was warm, and there was a weak pulse beat. *A heart. An actual heart. There is an actual heart trapped inside here.*"

A clue to the judge's predilections are given when our narrator reports seeing a phrase engraved "in a language I didn't know": ODI ET AMO. It is in Latin and usually translated, "I hate and I love." It has been more ominously translated, "I loathe her, I lust for her." The last translation may be especially germane go this story. The judge informs his guest that in his capacity as judge he sometimes encounters "a young woman like yourself, or a young man" who makes "a strong impression." Then the judge wants to know that person "more intimately" and "bring her, or him, into my life." Apparently, he easily justifies collecting their "hearts" since he loathes them as much as lusts for them.

The story ends with the woman "drowsy," perhaps from champagne, possibly from a drug slipped into it. She jokes that the drink "isn't a love potion, is it?' He answers, "I hope so." Grotesquerie can be this-worldly: "The Collector of Hearts" abuses his power for sexual exploitation. He plays havoc with those who are vulnerable since they have had legal troubles. In this story, Oates shines a powerful light on the way people at the margins, male as well as female, can be targeted by the respected and powerful.

Religiosity, Celebrity

"Demon" is told from the viewpoint of a psychotic youth (his mother frets he missed "his medicine") convinced his right eyeball has a pentagram in it that is the "Sign of Satan." He gouges out the eyeball. With the "sign of the demon" gone he falls to his knees "praying *Thank you God! Thank you God!* Weeping as angels in radiant garments with faces of blinding brightness reach down to embrace him not minding his red-slippery mask of a face. Now he's one of them himself, now he will float into the sky where, some wind-blustery January morning, you'll see him, or a face like his, in a furious cloud."

This eye gouging recalls Oates's novel, *Son of the Morning* that has a scene in which Christian evangelist Nathan Vickery gouges one of his own eyeballs out.

Why would this extraordinarily perverse act be repeated in Oates? Perhaps she is haunted by the grotesque implications of Jesus's saying: "If thy right eye offend thee, pluck it out." Indeed, that verse is troubling. Only four pages long, "Demon" masterfully carries the reader into the torments of a probably schizophrenic youth as underlines how easy it is for disturbed to obsess with religious imagery and even be destroyed by their religious (mis)interpretations.

"Elvis Is Dead, Why Are *You* Alive?" investigates the grotesqueries of celebrity obsession. It appropriately follows "Demon" for, as the latter delved into grotesqueries inherent in religion itself, this story explores how celebrity-obsession parallels religiosity and could even morph into a kind of religion. Meredith is a middle-aged married executive beset by dreams about being in a church where worshippers grieve for Elvis Presley. Meredith dreams the minister says the assembled group is there to mourn "our beloved Elvis who has passed over . . . Elvis our dead King is with [God], his soul in glory, and at peace, after the sorrows of this Vale of Tears."

Haunted by these dreams, Meredith looks at people, nagged by the question, "Elvis is dead: why are *you* alive?"

In one dream, Meredith and other mourners are handed scourges. They leave the church to attack other people, hacking at them with the scourges, shouting, "Elvis is dead, why are *you* alive?"

As the story closes, we read, "Meredith found himself on the cellar steps, descending the steps into the earthy-smelling darkness." He finds an item resembling the dream-scourges: "measuring perhaps fifteen inches in diameter, sickle-sized, made of an actual rug beater, razor blades and shards of wicked-looking glass clamped onto the heavy metal in a bizarre fan-shaped display." Meredith grips this instrument; the story ends. The reader is left to wonder if violence will follow because "Elvis is dead, why are *you* alive?"

In both stories, Oates explores the link between religious faith and the grotesque. They show how easy it is for faith to lead to violence. The second story raises questions about the nature of religious figures. Traditional religious figures can be viewed as akin to "celebrities"; modern celebrities are adored with a fanaticism easily shading into religious worship.

Haunting Family Folklore

Two stories in *Collector* are presented as family folklore. In both "The Sons of Angus MacElster" and "Shadows of the Evening," major events occur in the 1920s. The stories diverge since "Sons" is this-worldly crime fiction; "Shadows," an otherworldly horror tale.

"*A true tale of Cape Breton Island, Nova Scotia, 1923*" is the first sentence of "The Sons of Angus MacElster." A father of six sons, the is a hard-drinking sailor given to fisticuffs. Oates describes the confusion of his sons and the "hurtful old man we loved with a fierce hateful love, the heated love of boys for their father, even a father who has long betrayed them with his absence, and the willful withholding of his love, yet we longed like craven dogs to receive our father's blessing."

Angus goes too far, publicly assaulting his wife, bringing family disgrace. Our narrator, a son, recalls, "In his drunken rage Angus MacElster strips his wife of thirty-six years near-naked, as the poor woman shrieks and sobs," after which Angus heads for the barn to sleep among horses.

Their mother's public degradation leads the sons to ". . . in a fever of shouts and laughter we strike, and tear, and lunge, and stab, and pierce, and gut, and make of the old man's wind-roughened skin a lacy-bloody shroud and of his bones brittle sticks as easily broken as dried twigs . . . his blood gushing hot and shamed onto the straw and the dirt floor of the barn a glistening stream." The last sentence of the story: *This old family tale came to me from my father's father Charles MacElster, the eldest son of Cal.*" We know Cal as one of the six sons/murderers.

Oates shows a true understanding of the confused feelings so common to abused children when she describes how much these sons loved the father who routinely mistreated them. She also shows an understanding of how males are traditionally cast in both the roles of abusers and the opposite roles of protectors/defenders/avengers of women. Even as the sons take vengeance for their mother's humiliation, Oates shows that they imitate the abuser, having learned violence from him.

"Shadows" tells of the narrator's grandmother, Magdalena Schön, who, "in the late winter of 1928," when sixteen years old, was sent to live with a rich relative, her elderly and sickly aunt. Bored,

Magdalena takes a walk one afternoon. She hears a beautiful male voice singing, "*Now the day is over, night is drawing near, shadows of the evening.*" She finds the source is a singer in a Protestant church (Magdalena and her family are Roman Catholics and the 1920s were an era of high tensions between Catholics and Protestants. Although she feels she has "no business in the churchyard of a Protestant church," she is irresistibly drawn to the tenor. He is young and handsome and we are told she falls "in love" although she will never "acknowledge that fact."

Returning to the church, she finds things shockingly altered. The church is a "ruin" with "most of the roof . . . collapsed inward . . . covered in patches of moss." Equally altered is the man she loves: "grown skeletal," his face "wizened and sickly pale," eyes "narrowed to slits like those of a frightened, ferocious animal."

Magdalena rushes back to her aunt's house. A servant is appalled to see "her young face was lined and haggard" but opens the door upon recognizing the girl's voice. We are not told whether the alteration of young Magdalena was temporary or permanent but we know that the family was haunted by her experience through three generations. This story seems to me to play on the tension-attraction so often felt toward the strange and the "stranger." The singer is a mysterious man of an "alien" religion. It also plays with fears the young have about aging. Repulsed by her aunt, Magdalena thinks, "*I will never be so old! I will never be you!*" But the story tells us she lived to be a grandmother. Oates underlines the fear of aging is also underlined by the singer's sudden transformation from an attractive youth to "skeletal."

Both stories demonstrate how traumatic events are passed down through families, remembered by those who were not even alive to experience them.

Marked by Grotesquerie, Haunted by Marks

"The Affliction" and "Scars" tell how grotesquerie can be literally written on the body.

"The Affliction" tells of grotesquerie turned positive. A child is afflicted by a mysterious ailment causing "welts, clots, boils." He finds "bits of tissue and nerve, blood-threaded, sometimes opaque but more often semi-translucent, of the fluid-slippery texture of a jellyfish." He sees "swirls and arabesques in his flesh, bas-reliefs the size of half-dollars, constellations and peacocks' eyes, of every conceivable hue." Oates writes, "Where he'd always felt shame now he began to feel pride. For the *things* were his, his alone." He removes the growths, saves them, arranges them into designs, affixes them to surfaces, paints and sculpts over them. Through his affliction, he becomes an artist: "His secret! Did others have such secrets, were other artists similarly cursed, and blessed? . . . *We can admire and respect one another but never know one another: so be it,*" recalling what Oates calls the "most profound mystery of our human experience." It is likely "The Affliction's" protagonist is a character with whom Oates feels special kinship: they are both artists. The artist in the story transforms his "affliction" into paintings of arresting beauty. The ability to create something beautiful and powerful out of our wounds, physical or psychological, is vital to the creative process. Just as Oates, like any artist, uses painful truths to create superb fiction, the artist of "The Affliction" takes painful growths on his body as the basis for superb paintings. Perhaps one of the most profound mysteries of art is how often it is born of affliction, how artists are cursed yet blessed.

"Scars" enacts the fulfillment of a common fantasy, the dream of returning in triumph to those who wronged one "back when." "Scars" is about a celebrity visiting to her hometown. She is wealthy, famous, with agents to plan where she visits but we are not told if she is a writer like Oates or some other type of artist. Throughout the visit, she is reminded of youthful traumas. As a thirteen-year-old, she had a crush on an older teenager who disliked her. She was riding her bicycle and he -- deliberately, she believed -- turned in front of her with his car. She "swerved desperately to the side," fell, and was left with a "large sickle-shaped scar on my knee and other, fainter scars permanently etched in my flesh." Seeing the man in a crowd of well-wishers, she is "dismayed" to see the handsome youth who once warmed her virgin blood now overweight and balding. She thinks, *"You? You scarred me for life? . . . I adored you when you were nineteen, I don't adore you now, you have ruined everything I recalled of you."*

Escorted to a retirement home, she tries to "exude an air of intelligent interest" even as she is repulsed by elderly people lying "immobile in their beds" and the "stench of rancid food, aged and unwashed flesh, and stale urine." She experiences disappointment at seeing a teacher she feared in junior high school now reduced to a bedridden "obese sprawling shape." Haunted by the memory of how that teacher razzed her, leading the then-young girl to rush to a restroom where, "unable to see clearly," she put a hand through a pane of glass. Three decades later, the faint scars faint constitute "a graceful calligraphy in an unknown language." Instead of being heartened to see her old tormentor humbled, our protagonist is stricken with pity and embarrassment.

She recalls a high school bullying that turned physical, leaving her with scratches and cuts and how during it she thought: *"Why do you hate me? I love you."* After a speech, she sees her former tormentors applauding her and thinks, *"Why are you here, so changed? I loved you once, when you were hateful to me. I don't love you now, I feel nothing for you, now."*

"Scars" ends with the celebrity in her hotel suite. The event's hosts have given her a lovely floral display. She takes the bouquet to a window and tosses the flowers away. But she cannot toss away the grotesqueries of dismay and disappointment. The story ends with her marked by her return: "On my hands and bare forearms were sticky yellow pollen streaks, harsh as acid. Already my sensitive skin was reddening in streaks, as if scalded, already it was beginning to scar."

"The Affliction" and "Scars" can be viewed as mirror images as the former shows how damage to the body can be used for a greater good and the latter shows how damage to a person gets written upon the body.

Temple and Journey

"The Temple" is a tender story albeit grotesque in its tenderness. A woman believes she hears a faint sound from her backyard, reminding her of "plaintive mewing" together with a "muffled scratching, as of something being raked by nails or claws." She digs in the yard and finds "a human skull . . . hardly half the size of an adult's skull." She wonders: "had a child been buried here, it must have been decades ago, on her family's property?" She finds "scattered bones – a slender forearm, curving ribs, part of a hand, fingers." She takes them into her home, saying, "*I* am here, *I* will always be here . . . *I* will never abandon you." She arranges "the skull and bones into the shape of a human being." Her bedroom becomes a "temple" for the dead child. Oates deliberately leaves the story ambiguous as to whether the woman actually heard anything or just imagined it. We also do not know if the child was killed or died of natural causes. We do know a dead child's remains were consigned unceremoniously to the earth in an unmarked grave. The story is significant for the way Oates illustrates the odd similarity between a child whose life was cut short and a lonely adult who makes a private altar of the child's bones.

The final story in *Collector* is "The Journey." It is told from the viewpoint of a creature, species unclear, but a fantasy being. It opens: "How slowly the journey begins. Traversing the lush green landscape by inches. Weeks are required to cover mere miles." The readers learn that the "you" of the story is attracted to each "blade of grass, each sticky moist bud, blossom tendril, exposed root" but learns "not to suck them in your mouth." The creature cannot see the sun through the "snarled foliage overhead" and possesses "no word for sun." The journey's pace picks up until "miles can be covered within mere hours, hundreds of miles within days, thousands of miles within weeks. . . . The journey ends. Rolled up swiftly and efficiently behind you like a carpet, or a giant sheet of paper."

Just as Oates explored the intimate link between body and mind in the previously discussed stories, she explores the intimate link between the earth itself and its creatures — or possible creatures in "The Temple" and "The Journey." Both tales convey a strange sense of the sacred — or is that a sense that the sacred is itself inevitably strange? They raise questions that invite each reader's own answers.

Oates's Grotesqueries

These stories underline what Oates finds grotesque. "The Sky Blue Ball" is about how we are haunted by childhood yet, grotesquely, yearn to retrieve it.

The narrow entrance pressing of the "crouching," "squeezing," "squatting" characters of "Black Rectangle" represents how often people navigate, metaphorically and literally, life's tight areas for survival.

Jellyfish are prominent in *Collector*: live jellyfish for dessert in "Black Rectangle"; "The Affliction's" protagonist sees his skin growths as possessing the "fluid-slippery texture of a jellyfish." Other stories refer to seeing "damned jellyfish" and an area strewn with "seaweed, dead fish, jellyfish."

The jellyfish is a creature of delicate beauty notorious for the dangers of its sting. Its beauty and beastliness make it a fitting metaphor for life itself.

Another telling element of this collection is the frequency with which characters are in attics and basements. Lorraine Lake avoids a confrontation with Tippi through an attic trip; "Schroeder's Stepfather" and "Elvis" feature trips to cellars. Oates views the attic as ascending to a higher level of consciousness; the cellar the subterranean nature of the subconscious.

Collector displays Oates's fascination for the grotesque and understanding of what haunts.

Bibliography

Livesey, Margot. "Jellyfish for Dessert Again?" *The New York Times*. March 7, 1999.

Oates, Joyce Carol. *The Collector of Hearts: New Tales of the Grotesque*. Dutton. New York, NY. 1998.

Oates, Joyce Carol. *Haunted: Tales of the Grotesque.* Penguin Books. 1994.

Oates, Joyce Carol. *Son of the Morning.* Vanguard Press. 1978.

www.ingramcontent.com/pod-product-compliance
Lightning Source LLC
LaVergne TN
LVHW012027060526
838201LV00061B/4493